A WEDDING OF
HEARTS AND TIDES

NELLIE BROOKS

Merpaper Press LLC

Edited by Karen Meeus Editing

Published by Merpaper Press LLC

CONTENTS

CHAPTER 1

The sweet chime of the golden bell above the wooden door echoed through the air, and the rich, warm light of a late September day streamed into the small wedding dress store on Mendocino Island.

Hazel looked up from doodling a gown design on the empty page of her business ledger. Four middle-aged ladies were entering her store, laughing, talking, and juggling shopping bags and shoe boxes. The salty scent of the ocean and the subtle, sweet fragrance of blooming fall asters seemed to hug the friendly quartet.

Before the door fell shut again, Hazel caught a glimpse of the blue, shimmering ocean and the little bridge with the many small padlocks that led over the winding creek into Lover's Lane. She closed the book and set it on the counter.

Her mother and grandmother had kept ledgers like this, filling them with notes about their sales. But the long drought kept the tourists away, and most of the cream-colored pages were blank. Hazel rarely had occasion to jot down a price, a dress design, and a note about the happy customer who carried it out of the store.

The women turned to her expectantly.

"Welcome! How can I help you?" Smiling, Hazel rose from her stool, checking the single button of her suit's short peplum jacket and smoothing the skirt. She remembered her visitors well. Not long ago, Jenny, Faye, and Billie had brought their friend Ava here to find a dress for her recommitment ceremony.

Ava walked over to meet her. "Hi! Do you remember me?"

"Of course I do. Ava, isn't it?"

"Yes, that's right." Ava leaned forward confidentially. "Well, I had my recommitment ceremony. It was everything I hoped it would be."

"Congratulations! I'm so glad to hear that." Hazel had adored Ava's dress. It had been one of her best vintage pieces, preserved over many years in pristine condition. But much as she had loved seeing it on the mannequin by the big mirror, selling it paid the rent that month.

Hazel folded her hands on the counter. She couldn't resist the temptation to ask, "Did you enjoy wearing the dress?"

"*Loved* it. It was so comfortable. I felt beautiful, and let me tell you—" Ava broke into the biggest smile. "My husband got all starry-eyed when he saw me. That was... It touched me. I'll never forget it."

"Aww. That's great." Hazel wanted to know so much more. Had the fragile seam she'd fixed held up? Had the sequins and beading stayed where they belonged? What about the length?

But customers did not come to talk about seams and pearls and stitches. They came to talk about dreams and wishes, fears and hesitations, visions and hopes.

Her mother had ingrained that in Hazel early on.

So, instead of asking everything she wanted to ask, Hazel only smiled. It wasn't too hard; she was genuinely delighted that the dress had done its job and made Ava happy. Patiently, she waited to learn how she could help the four friends this time.

Ava gestured at her group, and they bustled closer, laughing and chatting. "We're back because now my friends need dresses. We have two weddings coming up."

"That's fantastic!" Hope lifted Hazel's head higher. *Two* dresses? If she could sell two dresses in one day, she would close early, take a walk on the bluff, and breathe a huge sigh of relief. She smiled at the women. "Thank you for coming back! Tell me how I can help you."

"I'm one of the brides." Faye, a petite, obviously pregnant lady with wavy brown hair, smiled back. "You've probably already spotted that I'm a problem case."

"Not at all," Hazel reassured her. Faye was not the first pregnant bride who'd walked into her store, and so far everyone had found a dress.

"And I'm the other bride." Jenny had also joined them. A blonde with kind blue eyes, she was taller than Faye.

"Congratulations on getting married! I'm happy to help you with anything you need." Already, Hazel's mind was churning, going over gowns that would show off Faye's delicate features and Jenny's elegant figure.

"Thank you." The corners of Jenny's eyes crinkled. "I'm not sure what I want, actually. I'd love to rummage around a bit on my own."

"Of course. Sometimes, that's the best way to discover your style." Hazel, in her heart, understood the female urge to run hands over delicate, soft fabrics in gorgeous colors and intricate beading to find *the one*.

Jenny thanked her and left, a light in her eyes. Ava followed her, also eager to rifle through the racks.

"I need help, please." Resignedly, Faye pointed at her swelling belly. "I always wanted to get a mermaid design."

"Oh." Hazel blinked. Her vintage fabrics were not as stretchy or elastic as modern ones. But she couldn't afford not to sell at least one gown today. And if it was between Faye's dress of the heart and keeping the store... Hazel bit her lip and nodded.

Mermaid it was. She'd have to tailor it to fit the belly and adjust the rest. Luckily, Hazel had inherited her mother's talent for sewing. She would make it work.

"Just kidding." Faye grinned. "I want an empire waist if you have it. Honestly, anything *but* a mermaid. I'd love something comfortable that doesn't pinch."

Relieved, Hazel exhaled and grinned back. "Then I have the perfect dress for you. Let me show you." She came out from behind the counter.

"What a gorgeous suit!" Faye exclaimed when she saw Hazel's full outfit. "Where did you buy this?"

Hazel laughed and put her hands on her waist, above the modest flare of the fitted jacket. "I made it myself. I'm a dressmaker. All the women in my family are. My great-grandmother founded this store to sell her designs."

"I love that. Do you make wedding dresses too?"

"I made one or two, once upon a time." Hazel hadn't been able to afford the expensive materials this year. Unlike the little suit she was wearing, the family patterns that had been handed down for generations called for frivolous amounts of beads and pearls, satin and lace. Luckily, to make ends meet, Hazel had started early on to sell gowns from other designers.

"Can I see one of your gowns?" Faye asked.

Hazel smiled. "I'm afraid mine sold already. But I still have a few dresses in the store that were made by others in my family. There is even one that my great-grandmother herself sewed. It's very beautiful but a difficult fit. I'm sure it was custom-tailored for someone who ended up not needing it after all." As she was saying the words, Hazel's gaze wandered to Jenny. Was she tall and slim enough to try it on?

"Faye, please stop talking and start looking." The last of the four friends, Billie Donovan, sat on the couch by the big mirror. "The sooner we get home, the better. I have a cormorant to feed."

Unbothered, Faye shook her head. "You know what *you* should do, Billie? You should look for a dress yourself. What if your handsome lighthouse keeper suddenly pops the question, huh?"

"Nah."

"He might. He's got that light in his eyes when he looks at you."

"What light?"

"You know, when they try to find the right moment."

"Oh...he does not." Billie blinked. "Does he? Do you really think so, or are you pulling my leg?"

"Well," Hazel interrupted gently. She remembered from the friends' last visit that Billie had a low tolerance for shopping. But when it came to wedding dresses, there was a surefire way of engaging a woman in the process. "If there's even the slightest danger of the question being popped... You know who would look absolutely gorgeous in a mermaid dress? *You* would."

"Me?" Billie's eyes widened. "Aren't those the tight ones?"

"Yes." Hazel smiled. "And you have the perfect curves for it. I saw it the moment you entered the store."

A thoughtful look came to Billie's eyes, and she rose, leaving her shopping bags by the couch. "Um—where are those? I might as well have a look while I wait for everyone else."

"Mermaid silhouettes are on the clothes rack to your left. Let me know if you like something, and I'll make a note to remember. It doesn't hurt to cover some groundwork before the time comes."

"Fine." Billie marched off.

"I have curves too," Faye complained. "Just not in the right places."

"You look great. Give me a moment to get you that empire I have in mind." Hazel gestured the way. "Let's have a look at what's hanging over there."

Hazel knew perfectly well where the dress for Faye hung.

But few brides—especially ones doubting the perfect dress existed at all—wanted the first sample they tried on to be *the one*. What if there was an even better one out there? Dress after dress was put on in the chase of that first high, and soon, the bride was utterly confused and exhausted.

"Let's see what we have," Hazel murmured. She pulled out a gown that was too snowy for Faye's complexion and another that was too frilly for her delicate frame. "How do you like these for starters?"

"I love them." Faye took the shiny fabric in her hands, admiring the beading and shimmering belts. "How pretty! Can I try them on?"

Satisfied with the reaction, Hazel nodded. "While you do that, I'll find the dress I really have in mind for you." She brought Faye to one of the two changing rooms and hung the dresses up. "Do you need help?"

"Um, thanks. I can still get in and out of my clothes by myself." Faye arched an eyebrow.

"I only wondered because of the zipper in the back."

The zipper had nothing to do with the reason Hazel had asked. A pregnant belly could throw off anyone's sense of balance, and the gowns were long and seemed to grow when putting them on. More than one lady—pregnant or not—had refused assistance only to trip and tumble, bumping her elbows and sometimes ripping the curtain off its curved rod.

But the customer was always right.

"I'll check in with you in a minute," Hazel promised.

"Okay." Faye disappeared into the room.

Ava appeared suddenly from behind a large vase of blooming autumn hydrangeas. "I'll stick around to help with the zipper," she whispered conspiratorially.

"Thank you," Hazel mouthed. Smiling, she made her way to the racks in the cozy window alcove. Without having to search, she parted the sea of frothy white, eggshell, and ivory and pulled out a gown.

Yes.

Perfect.

The muted ivory complemented the tone of Faye's skin. The soft pearl belt gently cinched in right below the bust, and the skirt cascading down in ethereal layers of chiffon perfectly accommodated a growing baby bump.

Contentedly, Hazel carried her prize back to the changing rooms.

"Can I try these on?" Jenny also arrived with two gowns on hangers.

"Absolutely." Hazel's eyes widened when she saw Jenny's picks. One of them was the store founder's vintage design that Hazel had mentioned to Faye. "You found one of my all-time favorites and the exact dress I meant to pull for you." Hazel gently lifted the delicate lace that overlaid the sweetheart neckline and reached to the shoulders. "It's a classic A-line silhouette, and this fabric drapes really gracefully. I can't wait to see you in it."

Hazel knew that Jenny would fall in love with the way the lace created an irresistible illusion effect to frame her collarbones and slender neck.

"I like the champagne color," Jenny remarked, turning the hanger to let the sunlight cast a subtle sheen on the fabric. "It's fitting since this is my second marriage."

"Imagine walking down the aisle," Hazel said softly. "Everybody is going to admire the effect of the lace above the silk train. It's such a focal point."

"I love a little train. Also, these sleeves are just perfect." Jenny tried to find a tag. "Who is the designer? We've been to a few stores, but I haven't seen anything like this."

"Actually, this is the last wedding dress my great-grandmother ever made," Hazel shared.

Jenny lowered the dress. "Really? Is it okay if I try it on?"

Hazel smiled. "That's why it is on the floor. Wedding dresses are for brides, not a hanger in a store. The only reason it's still here is because it's a difficult fit. It was clearly custom made, and it takes a very particular figure to pull off the lace in the back. It's impossible to change it without ruining the effect. Honestly, we haven't been willing to do that."

Jenny flipped her prize over to admire the intricate, hand-beaded flower motifs on the back. "I can see that. Goodness. I've never seen such beautiful lace."

"I'd be delighted if it fits. Would you like help?"

"Thank you, but I think I'm good." Jenny disappeared into her changing room.

A warm glow spread through Hazel at the thought of the gorgeous dress finally finding its bride. Smiling, she turned to Faye's curtain. "How is it going? Do you need anything?"

"I'm coming out." The curtain swung open.

Lifting her elegant, snowy skirt with both hands, Faye stepped out. "Well. Um. The first was way too poufy for me, with all the frills and ruffles. This one, I'm not sure. I think I like it?" She tugged on the sleeves and frowned at her reflection in the big mirror. "It's kind of what I want, but... I don't know. I'm not sure."

Hazel's professional eye immediately saw how the brilliant white of the fabric cast gray shadows on Faye's fair complexion. "Let's put it aside for now. I found the dress I was thinking of for you." She held it up. "The ivory color would go well with your skin, and there's no pouf. It's very delicate, and I think it would look wonderful on you."

"Oh!" Faye reached for the dress, her pupils widening. "Yes! *That's* the thing I was hoping for. Let me try it. Was this one made by someone in your family?"

"No, it's an Italian design." Hazel mentioned the name on the label.

"Never heard of them, but the longer I look at their dress, the more I like it," Faye replied cheerfully. "I'll try it." Her hand flew to her belly. "Oof. She's a kicker."

"Anything I can do?" Hazel smiled. She couldn't imagine how it felt to have a baby kick inside you.

Ava, who was watching from the small bench in the changing room, stood. "Come on, Faye. Waddle yourself back in here and sit for a second until the baby settles." She came to take the new dress from Hazel and then followed Faye back into the changing room.

"Good luck!" Hazel was in her early twenties. But she'd grown up in a wedding dress store and knew—simply *knew*—when a bride met her dress.

Faye was about to fall in love.

And the sale would help her stay afloat a little longer. Hazel sent out a quick, silent thanks when Jenny's curtain slid open.

Sometimes, there were these moments when the store seemed to fall silent, when the chatter of life ceased and the world took a happy little breath, glad for a moment that such things as brides and families and weddings existed.

Hazel clasped her hands together under her chin. "It fits you!" she breathed, her seamstress heart jubilant in her chest. After so many years of being ignored, the dress was finally allowed to shine.

"It wears like a dream," Jenny admitted and stepped in front of the mirror.

"It looks like it was made for you." Hazel agreed, marveling at the way the delicate lace stretched to perfectly show its beautiful motives.

"Oh, Jenny." Billie joined them. Her eyes started to shimmer, and she blinked at her friend. "You look stunning. Jon won't know what hit him."

Jenny turned this way and that in front of the mirror. "He'll love it. He'll absolutely love it," she whispered.

"Well then..." Hazel blinked her own reverie away. "I should ask the famous question, I suppose?"

Smiling, Jenny nodded.

Hazel inhaled. "Is this your dress?"

"Yes. Yes, this is my dress. I love everything about it."

"Congratulations! I'm so glad."

"Hazel, I'll take this one!" The second curtain swung back, and Faye stepped out. As soon as she spotted her friend, she clapped her hands together. "Oh Jenny! Wow."

Jenny laughed. "And you—you are *radiant*!"

Faye's eyes beamed as she joined Jenny in front of the mirror. "I haven't felt this pretty in years."

"You're not pretty, you're beautiful." Hazel smiled at her second bride. "So then, is it a yes for you too?"

"Yes!" Faye announced happily. "I only wish I could wear it out of the store right now. How can I put on my boring maternity pants when I look so good in this?"

"That choice is entirely up to you." Hazel allowed herself a wink. "Personally, I'm here for it."

"Ha, no." Billie shook her head. "Nope. You're not doing that." The women started to discuss the pros and cons of wearing gowns in everyday life, happily turning and admiring the beading and arranging the layers of the skirts as if the weddings were already here and it was time to walk down the aisle.

Hazel exhaled what was equal parts relief and happiness. She had needed this reminder that her job was the best in the world. But her job wasn't done yet. Trying to project the growth of Faye's baby, she set to work marking the hem of her dress. It needed shortening, but not so much that the growing belly would lift the hem too high. They'd need another fitting just before the wedding.

Jenny's dress fit just so. As long as Jenny's shape didn't change, the dress fit perfectly.

Once the marking was done and the ladies were busy changing back into jeans and sweaters, Hazel smoothed and returned the rejects that had to wait another day for their bride. Then she went to wait by the register.

Faye was the first to finalize her purchase. While Hazel hung the dress in her little atelier in the back to change it later, Faye pulled a card from her wallet and laid it on the counter. "I hope credit card is okay," Faye said when Hazel returned.

"Of course." Hazel took the card, routinely checked the signature, then ran it through the reader and printed out the sales slip. "Do you mind writing down your full name, phone number, and address for me?" She put a piece of paper and pen next to the receipt slip. "I always ask in case we'll need an emergency adjustment or delivery." She smiled at the memories of her customers' many last-minute predicaments. "I promise it has come in useful before."

"No problem." Faye wrote down her information and signed the receipt with a flourish. "Thank you! I'm glad I came here."

"And I'm glad you found your dress."

"The same goes for me." Jenny smiled and put her own dress on the counter. "I suppose I get to take it home now."

Smiling, Hazel spread out the fabric and pulled out silk paper to pack it up. "Still, leave me your information, Jenny. Not to jinx anything, but you never know what might happen."

"Here." Faye slid the paper and pen over to her friend.

"I never knew a dress could make me feel like this. Suddenly, I can't stop thinking about walking down the aisle. Or in my case, the beach." Jenny's face beamed as she opened her wallet. "I'd like to pay with a credit card too."

Hazel folded the gown into a large paper bag and took the card. "I love beach weddings. Which one do you have in mind?" There were dozens in the area, and all of them had seen their fair share of weddings.

Jenny finished jotting down her phone number and address. "Do you know the old hotel at Beach and Forgotten?"

The words froze Hazel's hand in midair. "The old mansion in the forgotten cove?"

"Yes, that's the one." Jenny capped the pen. "My family has lived there for generations. I'd like to get married on our beach."

With a shiver, Hazel unfroze. Softly, she set the card back down. Then she turned the paper to see the address Jenny had written down.

The old mansion was supposed to be empty and abandoned, the family gone from Mendocino Cove.

Hazel's heartbeat quickened as she recalled the promise she had made her mother to inherit the store. A promise that was supposed to be sheer formality. A quirky tradition, started by the store's eccentric founder and renewed each generation.

But nevertheless, a promise.

"Is something wrong?" Jenny tilted her head in question.

Hazel didn't know how to say the thing she had to say.

Slowly, she slid the credit card back across the counter to Jenny. Her mouth was dry. "I'm very sorry. I didn't realize who you were." She took the dress bag and softly set it behind the counter by her feet. Then she took a shallow breath. "I'm afraid I can't sell you this dress after all."

CHAPTER 2

"H ere we go. Freshly brewed and piping hot." Smiling, Jenny stepped out on the stone patio of the old mansion on Beach and Forgotten and lifted the carafe. "Who wants coffee?"

Both her guests wanted coffee. Jenny poured, adjusted the sun umbrella since the afternoon was sunny, and put a serving spoon next to the peach cobbler. Her duties done, she sat in one of the wide, comfortable wicker chairs.

Jenny had wanted to have her friends Christy and Agatha over for a while, and today it had finally worked out.

Before retiring, Christy had worked for an auction house in San Francisco and helped Jenny value some family heirlooms. Visiting Mendocino Cove, Christy fell in love with the wild beauty of Northern California's coast. When the small fixer-upper butting against that of her best friend, Agatha, came on the market, Christy did not hesitate to snap it up. Now, she was in town to sign the closing papers for her very own seaside cottage.

Jenny coughed and set down her cup. The hot liquid had burned the tip of her tongue.

"Easy. Here." Christy pushed a napkin over.

"Thanks." Gingerly, Jenny dabbed her mouth.

"She really said you couldn't buy the dress?" Agatha picked up the conversation they had started before Jenny left to make more coffee. Interestedly, the older woman propped her elbows on the table.

"Yes. She really did say that," Jenny confirmed.

Agatha shook her head. "There are so many wedding boutiques on Lover's Lane. Seems like this Hazel girl should be happy to sell you just about anything."

"I agree. It's peculiar," Christy added. "Why on earth would this girl put you in the dress, tell you it looks good, and then refuse your perfectly good credit card?"

"I don't know. I'm not sure she knew herself. But I was too confused to dig for an answer. We just left." Jenny lifted her coffee cup.

Three days later, she still vividly remembered how her joy had turned to ashes.

"I don't understand. The card is good," she had assured Hazel. "Besides, you just sold Faye her dress."

Hazel's voice sounded as incredulous as Jenny felt. "It's not the card. It's—I'm so sorry, but I can't sell you *any* dress. Maybe the store next door... They just ordered some new designs. You might find something there."

Jenny tucked her chin. "Are you serious?"

"I'm afraid so," Hazel murmured, lowering her eyes. "There are many other beautiful dresses in Lover's Lane."

"But I want this one."

"Um. It's, uh...I just can't sell it to you." The young dressmaker turned pale.

Jenny felt her ire rise. "And you forgot that when you were showing it to me?"

At this point, Billie put an arm around Jenny. Her eyes were blazing. "That's just not good enough, Hazel," she said sternly. "Obviously, it's for sale, like all the other dresses."

"I'm so sorry." Hazel's blanched cheeks blushed crimson under Billie's glare. "I really am."

"It's okay. It's okay. Come on, everyone, let's go." Taking Billie's arm, Jenny had turned and left.

A gull swooped for Agatha's lemon tarts on the patio table and she screamed, recalling Jenny to the present. Frowning, she set her coffee cup back down.

"Oh, dear," Agatha said, her voice full of pity. "It really got to you, didn't it?"

Jenny shook her head to get rid of the unpleasant memory. "Never mind." She exhaled. "It's just a dress. I'll recover."

"I wouldn't buy anything off the rack anyway," Christy said soothingly. "My tailor in San Francisco will make you a dress. What style are you looking for?"

"I don't know." Jenny shrugged helplessly. "I need it too soon to have it made. Besides, it's my second wedding. I wasn't even going to wear a big dress. Only this time...this time..." Her voice trailed off, and she pressed her lips together. She should never have pictured herself walking toward Jon in that dress.

But she couldn't stop.

"Goodness," Jenny said when she found her words again. She tried to laugh. "Look at me. I have everything I could possibly wish for and still cry over a dress. It's like I'm sixteen all over again."

"It's a *wedding* dress," Agatha said staunchly. "Second one or not."

"It's the thought of Jon," Jenny finally admitted. "I keep picturing his face as I walk down the aisle in this perfect dress and, well..."

"It's his first wedding, isn't it?" Christy asked gently. "That makes a difference."

Jenny nodded. "I wanted to make it special for him. But now I feel like going back to my original plan."

"What's that?"

"Getting married in jeans and a sweater, barefoot on the beach, hair blowing in the wind."

"That sounds good to me. That's what *I* would do," Agatha declared. "Though my hair is too thin to blow anywhere. And I no longer enjoy having sand between my toes."

Jenny half smiled, half sighed. "I don't mind sand between my toes. But Jon wants a *proper wedding*. He wants to invite all the cove and half the island. He is like that."

"No reason to despair. I'll call my tailor just in case." Christy patted Jenny's hand on the table. "Maybe he can whip you up something nice after all."

"I appreciate the offer, my dear. Thank you. But please don't call in any expensive favors on my behalf." Jenny smiled. "Remember that I'm a part-time adjunct professor with the salary to match. Jon is already paying for the wedding as well as the new house we are building in the vineyard. I want to at least buy my own wedding dress." She inhaled the warm, salty air, recalling her priorities. "It really is not a problem. I'll just have to have a look at other stores. I'm sure I'll find something else that fits."

"That's the spirit." Christy lifted her coffee cup in a cheer. "Of course you will find something. I have a few more days before I return to San Francisco. Maybe I'll come shopping with you and your friends."

"Maybe instead of bothering the girls, you'll schedule the plumber to have a look at your new cottage," Agatha said heartlessly. "Or do any of the hundred other things you need to do before you can move in. The place really isn't in livable condition."

Christy raised her eyebrows and shook her carefully curled coiffure. "I'm not going to rush anything, least of all the plumbing," she announced. "This cottage is my *project*. I want to take my time. In fact, I want to renovate it myself."

Agatha also raised her eyebrows. "You? With your own hands?"

"Of course with my own hands."

"With those fingernails?"

Christy wiggled her perfect manicure. "What about them?"

Agatha tilted her head. "Nothing. Not a thing. Only—" She was interrupted by the opening of the French door.

Smiling, Jenny looked up. The bickering of her retired friends had already distracted her from her disappointment over the dress, and when she saw who stood in the door, she truly forgot all about it.

Slowly, she pushed her chair back and rose. "River?"

CHAPTER 3

Her son grinned and stepped onto the patio. "They said I would find you here, Mom."

A small sound escaped the back of Jenny's throat as she ran over to hug River. "Darling! I didn't know you were coming! What are you doing here?"

"I told you I'd stop by and visit." He planted a kiss on her cheek.

"You didn't say when! I was waiting for your call," Jenny exclaimed, pulling him back in her arms. She still couldn't believe River was really here. For years, medical residency had taken up all his time. And just after it ended, his girlfriend left him. Jenny hadn't been surprised when her son had started to vaguely mention traveling. Europe, she had guessed. Or South America. Anything but Mendocino Cove.

"I wanted to surprise you. Wow, Mom, this place is *nice*. I've been missing out." Smiling, River freed himself to nod at Jenny's guests. "I'm sorry to barge in like this."

"Hello, young man." Christy nodded graciously.

"That's him then, is it?" Agatha asked Jenny. "He didn't go to Europe after all."

Jenny laughed. "Yes, this is my son."

"He's so handsome." Agatha patted the wicker chair beside her. "Sit by me, young man."

Jenny smiled at her son. "Go ahead, darling," she said and sat down herself. "Did you arrive just now?"

"I stopped at a little restaurant in town to ask directions to the hotel," River admitted and took the offered seat. He pointed at the coffee carafe on the table. "May I? I haven't had coffee this morning."

"Of course." Jenny poured him a cup and set a lemon tart on a fresh plate for him.

Agatha leaned over. "I understand you are a doctor."

River nodded. "Yes, ma'am. Freshly board-certified and ready to go. All I need now is a job."

"Oh, get a job at the local hospital, will you? They sure need another doctor. I'm tired of waiting for hours every time I have a cold." Agatha leaned back importantly. "If you do, I'll be your first patient."

"Do you have a cold now?" River's gaze became focused. "You do sound a little stuffy."

"If I had a cold, I wouldn't sit here and give it to your mom." Agatha shook her head. "It's my allergy; Christy brought her cat with her. Try the tart. Tell me whether you like it."

As directed, River took a bite. "Yum," he said, chewing. "It's delicious. I like it very much. Are you serious about the hospital looking to hire?"

"I know they need another doctor, but they're not hiring right now. If you want, I'll go over there and have a word with the people in the administration. Let them know we have a candidate in town. Who knows? Maybe they will hop to it and offer you a position."

River looked alarmed at the thought of Agatha telling the local hospital administration to hop to anything. "Please don't. I'm only visiting."

Jenny smiled. "We have so much to talk about, River. Where to begin?"

"Agatha, this is our cue." Christy rose. "We'll leave you to it. And Agatha, maybe instead of badgering the hospital administration, you can introduce me to that local plumber of yours."

Agatha's face fell at the turn of events, but she dutifully pushed back her chair and stood as well. "One doesn't just *introduce* someone to the local plumber," she fretted. "What do you think, Christy? It's not like he's sitting around at home, waiting for you to swan in with your cottage problems. There's always a *queue*. Besides, we don't really *have* a local plumber. The closest one is at least a half hour away. At *least*."

Jenny had barely inhaled a breath to say goodbye when she heard someone else step out on the patio. She turned to see that her daughter and her aunt, Audrey and Georgie, had returned from their walk on the bluff where they had picked flowers for the hotel.

"River?" Audrey ran to meet her brother, slinging her arms around his neck and squealing with surprise. "You finally came!"

"Yes, I finally came. Hey there, little sister. I hear you are a real grown-up hotel manager now." River hugged Audrey and kissed the top of her head.

Jenny rose and went to meet Aunt Georgie, whose arms were full of bright, blooming California asters. "Do you remember River?"

"Last time I saw him, he was still in diapers." She walked up to the siblings. "I'm Aunt Georgie."

Strictly speaking, Georgie was Jenny's aunt. But everyone under fifty simply called her Aunt Georgie.

River smiled and offered his hand. "Hello, Aunt Georgie. I've heard a lot about you."

Aunt Georgie pulled a yellow aster from her bouquet and pressed it into River's palm. "I'm sure you did, darling," she said as River's fingers closed around the flower. "But I'll eat my hat if it was good."

"Of course it was good." Jenny went back to the table and lifted the coffee pot. "Let's all sit down and talk. Who wants lemon tarts?"

Everyone wanted lemon tarts, and Agatha and Christy, happy to stay a little longer after all, started to quiz River about his education.

His answers were animated and funny, making everyone laugh. Listening to their back and forth, Jenny relaxed in her chair until her daughter's low voice beside her caught her attention.

Audrey patted Aunt Georgie's hand. "So, do you approve of my brother?"

Aunt Georgie weaved her head. "I suppose. I haven't talked with him yet."

When Audrey raised a stern eyebrow, her aunt relented. "He's probably a good egg."

"He really is." Audrey leaned back. "You know, I'm secretly glad he didn't get engaged."

"You are, are you?" Aunt Georgie looked up. "Why?"

"I never once felt like his ex was the one for him." Audrey tilted her head. "Don't get me wrong. She was nice enough, and I get why he proposed. But I also understand why she said no and skipped out on him. They didn't really vibe."

"What about yourself? I guess there aren't any young people around in the cove."

"I'm too busy getting the hotel ready for guests." Audrey checked her phone. "By the way, my friend Zoe is young people. She'll be here any minute."

"Zoe lives in Seattle," Aunt Georgie pointed out. "She only comes to Mendocino Cove to visit her parents."

"Well, I'm glad she does. She offered to help me check out the attic today. The hotel still has to pass the fire inspection."

Aunt Georgie raised a querulous eyebrow. "*Another* permit? Running a hotel did not used to be so complicated."

Audrey smiled. "You mean back in the sixties and seventies? You're probably right about that."

A car engine came humming down Forgotten. It was barely audible over the rolling of the Pacific Ocean, but Audrey had clearly been waiting for it. She pushed back her chair and stood. "We also have to make the hotel wheelchair accessible."

"Is that really necessary?" Aunt Georgie looked put out.

"Of course it is. What are people in wheelchairs supposed to do otherwise? We'll put a ramp by the small parlor. You won't even notice the difference." Audrey waved for her brother's attention. "River, how long are you staying?"

He looked over. "I don't know yet. To be honest, I have no firm plan."

"Stay as long as you can," Jenny said quickly. "The longer, the better. Maybe you really can find work here."

"Do you think so?" River asked.

"It doesn't hurt to introduce yourself at the hospital." Stranger things than unexpected job offers had happened in Mendocino Cove.

Audrey went to hug her brother in his chair. "I'll see you later. We'll catch up tonight, drinks in my room. I want all the dirty details."

"On what?" Grinning, River brushed his dark hair back.

"You tell me, doctor." Audrey smiled brightly, and then she went inside to meet Zoe.

CHAPTER 4

Zoe had already let herself in and stood in the kitchen, drinking a glass of water. Audrey was glad her friend felt as comfortable in the old hotel as in her parents' beautifully restored arts and crafts home.

"Hi." Audrey joined her. "Good to see you. Thanks for helping me tackle the attic."

"I wouldn't miss it for the world." Zoe smiled back and washed out her glass, setting it on the wooden dish rack to dry. "I brought extra trash bags and gloves." She pulled a scrunchie from her wrist and tied back her hair.

"Excellent. How much longer are you in town? Am I hogging you?" Audrey asked and fished a bucket out from under the sink.

"It's fine," Zoe assured her. "If I don't keep busy, I'll start thinking about my life in Seattle. And I don't want to think about it if I don't have to."

Audrey squirted dish liquid into the bucket and turned on the faucet, watching as the steaming hot water churned the soap into foam and bubbles. "Is your job at the bakery still stressful?"

Zoe nodded, a small line between her eyes. "Last week, my boss scheduled me without asking. I had to miss a concert I'd been looking forward to for months so I could pull a double shift for him. I love being a baker, but not like that. I can't do this much longer."

"I'm sorry."

Zoe was the nicest, most helpful person Audrey knew. Unfortunately, her unscrupulous boss knew it too. "They're taking advantage of you."

"A little bit." Zoe pursed her lips. "Or lately, a lot."

Audrey turned off the water. "Zoe, let's not clean the attic. Let's go have an ice cream and a walk on the beach instead, okay? I don't want to take advantage of you too."

Zoe looked up, surprised. "This is different. You asked. And I said yes. Besides, I just spent two days eating muffins and staring at the horizon. I'm bored to tears. Don't try to keep me out of your unexplored attic. What will we find?" She smiled. "Treasure? Rats?"

"Not *rats*, I hope. Raccoons, possibly, or bats. Treasure, maybe." Audrey smiled back. "If dusty lace-up boots and spooky dollhouses count."

"They count. What are we waiting for?" Zoe grabbed her trash bags and plastic cleaning gloves. "Let's go!"

"All right. Follow me." Audrey hauled the bucket out of the sink and slung a clean kitchen towel over her shoulder. "We'll be the first to go up there in, oh...at least thirty years, I suppose. Maybe more. Maybe much more." Doing her best not to spill the soapy water, she led the way into a small, white-washed room off the kitchen and switched on the light. "This is the staircase that leads to the attic." She looked up the old wooden stairs that ended in the black square of a closed trapdoor.

Zoe ran a finger over a stair and held it up, showing Audrey the dust. "You're not lying when you say nobody has gone up there in years."

"I never lie," Audrey lied and primly squared her shoulders. "Ready?"

"Ready," Zoe confirmed.

Audrey tested the creaking staircase when the faint sound of laughter drifted in from the patio. "Does your mom have guests?" Zoe asked.

Audrey, convinced the old stairs would carry them, told her friend about River's return as they made their way up the stairs. When she reached the trapdoor, Audrey knocked experimentally on the boards above her head. The deep, low taps sounded solid. At least they didn't have to worry about rotten wood or falling through weak spots in the floor.

"Be careful."

"I will. Here, hold the bucket while I try to open this." Audrey lowered the bucket down to Zoe.

Water spilled, dousing Zoe's arm. "Hey, watch it," she muttered and pushed up the wet sleeve of her sweater before taking the bucket and balancing it as best she could.

"Sorry." Audrey took another step so she could brace her shoulder against the wooden door. Straightening her knees, she pressed. "This thing is heavy."

Zoe peered around her. "Is it locked?" She squinted into the dark.

"It's just stuck. I can feel it loosening a bit." Audrey pulled a big breath into her lungs and readjusted her stance. On the exhale, she pressed upward again. "Ugh!" Her effort was rewarded with a groan of wood and metal, and then, slowly, as if unwilling to give away its secrets, the trapdoor lifted.

Carefully, she tipped the door up until she heard it click into position. "Uh. Suddenly I don't like poking my head into the attic. What if there's somebody there, looking back at me?"

Zoe grinned. "Like who? Your great-grandpa's ghost?"

"What if it's a rabid raccoon?"

"You have a doctor in the family," Zoe said. "So, no worries."

"No worries," Audrey repeated. She took another step and looked into the attic.

"What? What do you see?"

Zoe's nervous tone made Audrey chuckle. "I see a lot of stuff stacked everywhere. The light is kind of dim though, and there are plenty of dust motes in the air." She coughed, waving her hand in front of her face. "I should have brought a lamp."

"Really? I saw a couple of skylights from the outside."

"They must be blind with dust or age. Maybe we can clean them up. Hang on." Holding on to the trapdoor opening, Audrey turned as best she could, making sure no glowing eyes or suddenly moving objects were coming her way. But it was quiet, and warm, and unexpectedly peaceful under the slanted roof. And big. Vast, really. Audrey couldn't see either end of the attic, and even the gable was far above her.

She pulled herself into a sitting position. "The floor is solid," she called down.

"Oh, was there a doubt about that?"

"No, not really." Audrey stood and stamped on the boards. "It's fine. Good, because I still need a structural permit too."

"You sure it's good?"

"Come on. I'll take the bucket." Audrey squatted to reach for it. The little bit of hot, soapy water wasn't going to clean the grime up here. They'd need a firehose for that.

Zoe hauled herself into the attic. "Whoa. It's huge."

"I know. Look at all that stuff." Audrey put her fingertips to her temples. "It'll take a lifetime to clear out."

"Yeah," Zoe said enthusiastically. "I'm sure you can use lots of it, though. All those rugs over there!" She marched straight to a low pyramid made of long rolls and flapped back a corner. "Wow. Audrey, this is the real deal."

Audrey joined her friend. The rug had been rolled up, protecting the now-exposed pile from the dust. Despite the hazy skylights, the pattern showed bright gemstone colors. "I don't know much about rugs," Audrey murmured, running a hand over the soft weave. "But this would be expensive to buy."

"For real," Zoe said and let the corner flop back. "I went shopping with Mom for their house here, and we didn't even dare to look at the antique rugs."

"Well, now you can have some of these." Audrey looked around. "How are we going to get them downstairs, though?"

"We'll ask the men for help." Zoe wiped her hands on her jeans.

Audrey nodded. "It'll be a community effort. What's this?" With her fingertips, she lifted a heavy cloth that was draped over a tall form and pulled. In a cloud of whirling motes, the cloth dropped to the ground.

"Ah!" Zoe coughed into her elbow. "It's a mirror!"

"Beautiful." Audrey touched the smooth frame. The shimmering, warm wood looked new, even though the silver under the mirror glass had some tarnished specks. "That's mahogany, isn't it?"

"I have no idea. It's something nice. Goodness, Audrey, I think you have more of a treasure trove than a fire hazard up here."

"I'm starting to think so too. Aww, I want this mirror downstairs."

"You'll have to call in even more men for that. It looks heavy."

"Yeah." Reluctantly, Audrey let the beautiful piece go and turned to another bulky, shrouded form.

Moving sometimes slowly, sometimes quickly, they went through the attic, peeping under drape-covers and cloths, discovering oil paintings of sailing ships and angry seas, fine furniture for the guest bedrooms downstairs, and all sorts of antiques.

"Look at the suitcases." Zoe pointed. "This one's almost as long as I'm tall." She tapped against it, listening to the sound. "There's something inside."

"Let's open it and see." Audrey squatted beside the old shipping trunk. She pried the metal clasps loose and wiggled the lid until it lifted.

"What is it? A skeleton?" Zoe asked with a smile on her lips and worry in her voice.

"Just old clothes." Audrey rocked back on her heels. "A *lot* of old clothes. These trunks are enormous. I'm definitely taking one of them on my next trip."

"Coastal Airlines says no, you don't." Zoe giggled and went to another chest-like trunk that stood below one of the narrow skylights. "May I?"

"Go ahead." Audrey lowered the lid again, wondering to whom it had belonged. Maybe even Phoebe Seabrook of Nantucket, the family's original matriarch? Audrey wasn't firm on the history of trunks through the ages.

"Also clothes," Zoe reported. "Oh, Audrey, blouses with poufy sleeves. I love it!" She unfolded a shirt that was stiff with age and starch, revealing neatly pressed pleats and a high collar. "Come, look at these mother-of-pearl buttons."

"I'm trying to shut this, but it's stuck. Why won't it go—" Audrey pressed the lid down, but still it didn't go down low enough to snap closed. "Hmm." She opened the lid again and tapped the flashlight app on her phone to inspect the silk that lined the trunk. "There's something wedged in there." She reached out and ran her fingers over the smooth lining until she felt a slight, flat bulge. Whatever was hidden there had slipped too close to the hinge.

"Hey, I think it's a book." Audrey shone her light along the seam until she found a thin, long rip. She leaned in. Not a rip—a cut. The edge was clean and had no loose threads. Had somebody made themselves a secret compartment? "Zoe?"

"What?"

"I think someone hid it on purpose."

"Someone hid a book?" Zoe folded the old blouse back into the chest and joined Audrey, who was trying to wiggle the thin book out of the lining. "What sort of book?"

CHAPTER 5
The Past

Marianne, dressed in the new tea gown with the dropped waist, flowing layers, and embroidered flowers, looked down the staircase. The voices told her that Mama's guests had arrived. She heaved as much of a sigh as her corset allowed.

But Tessie still tied them too tight, and for a moment, Marianne felt faint. Her heart was beating hard from rushing back home and dressing in a hurry. Naturally, the ivory buttons had forever refused to go through their holes. Her windswept curls had refused to be pinned. And Tessie, on top of tying the corset too tight, had refused to be nice and instead scolded Marianne for being tardy.

Marianne had wanted to stay in her room more than anything. Eat a slice of poppyseed cake. Read a book by the open window. Inspect the new fossil she'd just collected on the beach. Not talk to guests. That sort of thing.

But of course, that was impossible.

After all, the guests had come specifically to see her. In the new tea gown, with pinned curls and pretty buttons.

Down the corridor, a door opened. Tessie leaned out for a moment, her blue eyes and red face glaring a warning.

"I'm going! I'm going," Marianne whispered. She straightened her back and tried to feel elegant and graceful. Like a young lady of marriageable age, eager to meet her destined suitor.

She exhaled a huff. It didn't work. No feelings of elegance at all. Maybe she'd been out on the wind-blown cliffs too long after all, and it had addled her brain just as Tessie said.

Resigned, Marianne lifted her long skirt. One of these days, she'd stumble to her death because she couldn't see her feet for swirling fabric.

Maybe not on the stairs. But on a cliff? Sure. Every step you took could kill you if your foot slipped.

"Why can't we wear trousers already?" Marianne muttered under her breath as she pictured herself lying crumpled on the bottom of a cliff, the victim of her long skirt.

"Marianne? Darling?" Mama called.

Marianne startled.

"Marianne? Marianne, darling, where *are* you?" Mama sounded particularly cheerful. It was a sign of danger.

Robert seemed as good as any other man. He looked nice enough, and he owned a small sawmill. It would grow, his mother had promised. In a few years, they would be wealthy.

The talk in town was that the new mill would never be able to compete with the Donovans' lumber business. But Marianne wasn't worried. They'd always have her dowry.

"Darling? Right *now*." An edge sharpened Mama's voice.

It needed to be done, even if her pumping heart told her that it wasn't safe.

"I'm coming. Coming!" Grabbing the railing, Marianne hitched her skirt and quickly went downstairs.

Mama didn't enjoy waiting. She was born on a ship, hey-ho, and while she was every inch the lady Marianne wasn't, Mama *would* behave like an old sea captain when it suited her.

Not that Marianne was going to complain. Mama would only tell Grandmama, who *was* an old sea captain. Mutiny wouldn't do.

"*Mari*—Ah! There you are, darling. What kept you so long? Come here." Mama surveyed her quickly and, to Marianne's relief, nodded. She was satisfied. "Say hello to our guests, dear."

"Hello," Marianne said and winked at Robert.

He raised an eyebrow and pushed a finger under his collar, pulling it away from his neck. Marianne would have done the same if she'd had to squish her poor throat into that stiff thing.

Robert's mother, Klara, put a hand on his arm to stop his boyish behavior. "Well, I'm glad you could finally join us, Marianne," she said in a voice that was higher than usual. "Robert?" Her grip on his arm tightened, bunching the fabric of his sleeve.

"Hello, Marianne." His lips curled into a smile. "You look swell. Erm. Enchanting."

Enchanting. Marianne bit her lip so she wouldn't laugh out loud. The corners of her mouth lifted, nevertheless.

Robert's eyes narrowed.

Quickly, Marianne smoothed her face and said, "Thank you, Robert. How kind of you to say so."

She folded her hands and glanced at her mother. "Are we going to sit outside, Mama?"

After her morning climb, Marianne was positively starving. She'd found an ammonite but missed lunch. Tessie had mentioned there were freshly cut strawberries with sugar and whipped cream waiting in the kitchen.

Instead of answering, Mama only smiled. Maybe it was too early for the strawberries.

"My dear Klara," Mama said to Robert's mother. "I am dying to show you the October asters I planted. Would you mind looking at them and telling me how pretty they are?"

"I'd love to," Klara declared and took the arm Mama offered. "I was just thinking I'd like some asters myself if it weren't for the salty air on the island."

Klara glared at Robert and Mama glared at Marianne, and off their elders went.

"I wasn't aware of any new asters," Marianne said after a while. "Do you want some strawberries, Robert?"

"I want some *air*," he said and pulled on his collar again.

"Your cravat is too tight. Here, let me help you." She went to him, but when she raised her hands to loosen the knot, he stepped back.

"Never mind my cravat," he muttered. "Marianne, you know why they left us alone, don't you?"

Marianne looked at the ground. She'd known he would talk to her today. And while it felt like a hundred buckets of awkwardness, she also knew well enough that she had to listen, smile, and say yes.

"Yes, I do," she murmured, no longer hungry.

"Well then...how about it?"

Marianne arched an eyebrow. Maybe she *was* a tomboy. Maybe she liked climbing the cliffs and hunting for fossils better than sitting around in pretty dresses and curled hair. But that didn't mean she was Robert's *chum*. Mama had done her bit to raise Marianne properly. "How about *what*?"

"Will you marry me? Come on. Just say yes and we can go outside. It's so stuffy in here."

"Oh." Somehow, Marianne had thought Robert would be more tender. Maybe a longing look into her eyes or a stutter because he loved her so much.

"You like to make a fellow wait, don't you?" He looked her up and down in a way that made her blink with shock. "Well, pretty little thing like you can do that, I suppose. Though I don't think it's kind, exactly. Especially when I'm so warm."

Marianne's eyes widened. She had heard the stories about taming husbands. All the married girls told them. But none of them had whispered about being called a *thing*, pretty or not, when they got engaged.

But maybe it wasn't the sort of news they would share? Marianne did want to be kind, and she did want a house of her own. "Um." She cleared her throat. "I don't mean to make a fellow wait, but...yes. I suppose."

"Oh, you suppose you want to marry me, do you?" Now he came closer, standing right in front of her, with his collar digging a red line into his neck. But at least he was smiling now—and Marianne liked his smile.

"Yes, I suppose I do want to marry," she said and smiled back.

"Ask me," he said, lowering his face to hers. "It's your turn to ask me."

Marianne had no choice but to put her head back if she wanted to keep looking at him. "Ask you what?" she asked, trembling. It was strange to have his face so close to hers. She could smell his hair pomade and his dental powder.

"Ask me if *I* want to marry *you*," he murmured, his breath brushing her cheek.

"Um. Do you want to marry me?" Marianne tried to turn her head because the dental powder was overwhelming. What did he have in there? Cardamom? Cloves? Cloves. *Ugh*.

"Yes. Yes, I do. Kiss me."

Marianne swallowed, closed her eyes, tried not to think, and kissed Robert.

Robert's lips were as soft and wet as fresh fish.

She'd kissed a boy before. Secretly, on the beach, when she was sixteen. She'd scraped her leg raw climbing the cliff, and he had found her. He built her a fire and used his own shirt to bandage her wound when she was settled. He caught her a fish to grill. His name was Mateo, and his eyes had been black, like the hot glowing coals in his fire. His lips had been firm, salty like the ocean, sun-warm, and full of longing.

Mateo had not stayed in the cove. He had been on his way to Monterey, where he meant to find work in the fields.

Marianne did not miss Mateo. But for two years, she remembered his kindness and his kiss.

"Good. Then it's done." Robert straightened. His lips had not returned the pressure of her lips to his.

Marianne blinked her eyes open again. "That's it? That's all?"

"I already talked with your father. I have his blessing. So...yes. I guess that's it. We're a done deal." Rob nodded, looking satisfied, and took her hand. "Oh, I forgot." He fished a ring from his vest pocket and showed it to her. It had a small diamond in the center. "Here." He slipped it on her hand. "Don't I get a thank you?"

"Thank you. It's very pretty," Marianne said mechanically.

"That's right. Now let me look at my bride." He raised her hand and arm as if he expected her to twirl like a figurine in a music box.

Confused, Marianne pulled away. Suddenly, she found it hard to breathe. And she desperately wanted to shield herself from Robert's penetrating gaze.

Papa never looked Mama up and down like that. But maybe that sort of look was another secret married women did not share?

Blushing hot when Robert's eyes crawled back to her chest, Marianne tugged her hand from his and turned away. "Mama?" she called out in a wavering voice, determined to end the tête-à-tête. Robert had never before been so strange. "Mama? Please come. I have good news."

Relief flooded her like a warm tide when her mother called back immediately, appearing around the corner of the terrace as if she'd been waiting. "Darling, good news?"

"She said yes," Robert reported proudly before Marianne could take another breath.

"Oh, my dear. I'm so happy!" Mama came to kiss Marianne, which was a good thing because Robert finally had to let go of her hand.

"I will be so delighted to call you my daughter," Klara announced and, after kissing her son, came to do the same to Marianne.

"Thank you," Marianne mumbled.

Klara kissed the offered cheek and straightened. "Magda, do you know what I'll do?"

"What is that?" Mama was still fondly looking at Marianne.

"I will make your daughter the finest wedding dress of them all," Klara declared. "I will make sure that Robert has the most beautiful bride ever to marry in Mendocino Cove."

"Oh." Mom folded her hands under her chin. "Klara, what a generous gift!"

"Thank you, Mrs. Rowley," Marianne said quickly, catching her mother's eye.

"You deserve nothing less," Klara said and patted Robert's arm.

A small line, just deep enough for the discerning eye of a daughter, formed between Mama's eyes. "I'm sure Marianne won't disappoint," she said, a drop of coolness in the words. "Why don't we all sit down and have some strawberries and sweet cream?"

Klara smiled widely, unaware of the change in Mama's mood. "That would be lovely," she said happily. "Thank you. I'm quite dizzy with happiness."

Mama took Marianne's hand into her own, glancing at the new diamond ring but not mentioning it.

"Please have a seat, dear Klara, Robert." She ushered Marianne ahead of her toward the kitchen. "My daughter and I will be back in a moment."

CHAPTER 6

T he ringing of the doorbell made Hazel look up
from her novel. After last week's debacle with
Jenny, not a single customer had set foot in the store.

"Hi, Hazel." Faye peeked through the gap in the
door. "Are you open?"

"Yes. Yes, the store is open. Please come in." Hazel
put her book on the shelf under the counter and
rose from her stool. Her smile felt strained. The
embarrassment from the week before came flooding
back, heating her neck.

Faye entered, closing the door behind her. She
brought with her the scent of salt and sea. "Hey."

Hazel put her hands on the counter. The feeling
of the warm, smooth wood under her fingertips cen-
tered her, and she felt her smile soften. "I'm glad you
came."

Faye walked over to her. She was wearing a pretty,
knee-length maternity dress and held a grocery net
filled with the white paper flowers that the store across
the street sold as wedding decor. "I know I'm back
earlier than we agreed on," Faye said. "But I was passing
by and thought I'd stop by and check in." She set her

net full of flowers down. "How are the dress alterations going?"

"Just fine. In fact, the dress is ready. Would you like to try it on now?"

"Sure." Faye looked surprised. "You do work fast, don't you?"

Rounding the counter, Hazel shrugged. "Honestly, I didn't have anything else to do."

"Hmm." Faye followed her to the back of the store. "Have you reconsidered selling Jenny that wedding dress she liked so much, by any chance?"

"I can't."

"And have you thought more about telling us the reason?"

Hazel stopped and closed her eyes to take a breath. "I was just so surprised last time that I didn't know what to do." She turned around to look at the older woman. "I'm really embarrassed about it."

She expected Faye to frown, but the older woman's smile only deepened. "Tell me what happened."

"Before she gave me the store, my mother made me promise never to sell our wedding dresses to the family that lived in the forgotten cove. She told me she had made the same promise when she inherited the store. So did my grandmother."

Faye's eyes widened. "What a strange promise."

"I know. Mom was very sick by the time she asked for it, so I didn't argue or ask. I didn't want to upset her, and I didn't think it mattered since nobody lived in the forgotten cove anymore. I thought the promise was just an eccentric tradition. I should have been more careful." Hazel rubbed her cheek. "I'm so sorry. I can't do anything about it."

"You can't, or you won't?" Faye asked, but a small smile reassured Hazel that she wasn't angry.

Hazel pressed her lips together. She had lain awake at night, mulling over that question. "I suppose I wouldn't exactly lose the store again if I broke my promise now. And I really can't stand it when people are mad at me."

Faye nodded. "But?"

Hazel shrugged helplessly. "It's my mother. She raised me, she taught me everything she knew, and in the end, she gave me this store. I love her, and I miss her every day. I owe it to her to keep my word."

"That I can understand," Faye said gently. "I still miss my mother every day too. And I wouldn't break a promise to her either."

Hazel nodded gratefully. The women in her family all had their children late in life and left them too soon. If Hazel had a choice, she would have her kids while she was still young. She wanted to be there for them as long as they needed her.

"Well, if it's like that...Jenny understands these things too," Faye said. "You should have told her. Not that missing out on a dress rocks her foundation. But knowing the reason would have made it easier."

"I realize that now, but I wasn't thinking clearly," Hazel said miserably. "I'm sorry. Please tell her for me."

Faye sighed. "Actually, I was going to ask if you'd sell the dress to me. Then I was going to give it to Jenny. But now I won't do that. I don't want you to break your promise, and Jenny wouldn't thank me for it either." She tilted her head. "Nobody wants you to feel bad, Hazel."

"Thank you." Hazel moistened her lips. "Thanks for being so understanding. I know the promise seems stupid and sentimental. But I can't change how I feel."

"We all have stupid, sentimental things that are important to us," Faye said kindly. "Don't worry. It isn't the last dress in the world, and Jenny isn't angry. She will simply find something else to get married in."

Grateful, Hazel nodded. Explaining herself to Faye felt good.

Like a boulder off her heart.

Not only because she hated disappointing a woman who'd found her perfect wedding dress. Word of mouth traveled fast and could quickly kill an already struggling business in the small world of Mendocino Island. But Faye was being so kind; maybe the fact that not a single customer had come to the store since the dress debacle had really just been a coincidence.

Hazel inhaled, feeling her lungs widen for the first time in a while. "I'll go get your dress now." She hurried into her atelier to get it, giving the gown a last inspection as she carried it back. She had snipped all the loose threads, and the intricate beading was firmly and invisibly stitched in place. Dresses for pregnant brides could be tricky, but the empire waist on this one made adaptations easy.

"Here it is." She showed the dress to her customer, lifting the pillowy hanger high so the softly layered skirt fanned out.

"Ooh. It's even prettier than I remembered." Faye touched the cascading fabric longingly. "Can I try it on right now?" She put her hands on her belly, defining its shape under the wide blouse.

The baby had clearly had a sudden growth spurt since the fitting. Sometimes, it happened quickly. Hazel had heard plenty of stories about pregnant brides who no longer fit in dresses that had been fine only days before.

Hazel smiled. "If you don't mind." It would show her how much growth the layers could hide. Already thinking about seams and beads and the strategic placement of satin ribbons, Hazel hung the dress into the bigger changing room and swept the curtain open for her bride. "Do you need help?"

"Nope, I'm good."

"I'll be at the counter. I want to check the measurements I wrote down in case it's too tight now and we need to let it out a bit more."

"I'm exactly the same size as last week," Faye muttered and stepped into the changing room.

"Of course." Hazel smiled. The conflict between wedding dressmakers and pregnant brides was surely as old as humanity itself. She dropped the curtain. "Let me know if you want me."

CHAPTER 7

The waist would let out another inch before messing with the pattern of beads.

Hazel rubbed her chin, thinking. Faye carried low. That was in their favor.

Abruptly, she looked up from the measurements scribbled on the paper. That had been a *loud* bump. More than an elbow hitting the wall of the changing room. Hazel put down her pencil and stood. "Faye? Is everything good?"

"Hazel? Hazel!"

She turned on her heel and sprinted back to the dressing room. The curtain rod was torn down, and Faye lay, half in, half out of her new gown, on the floor.

"Oh no, are you all right?" Hazel kneeled beside Faye, pulling the curtain off her.

"The baby!" Faye groaned. "I fell on my belly."

"I'm sure you're okay. You're okay," Hazel said frantically, taking hold of Faye's arm. "What hurts?"

"My hip. And my head. I hit my head going down. Ouch. Don't—my ankle!"

Hazel exhaled a tense breath. "Stay where you are for a moment. I'm going to pull the dress off of you so you can move your legs."

"Yeah." Faye's hands went to her belly. She whimpered, making a pitiful sound full of fear. "I hope she's all right! I fell hard."

"We'd better get you to the doctor." Hazel tucked the dress over Faye's ankles, trying not to snowball. Surely the baby was okay? The baby *had* to be okay. "I should have stayed to help—"

"I don't know why I lost balance," Faye interrupted her tearily. "Ouch. My ankle *really* hurts. Careful."

"Sorry." Clumsily, Hazel wiggled the last of the dress out from under Faye. "There." She tossed the dress aside and kneeled beside Faye, helping her to sit. "Your belly has had a growth spurt since last week. You might not even have noticed, but dressmakers have an eye for these things. Your center of gravity shifted. Maybe it threw you off balance." She rocked back. "I'll call an ambulance."

"If there isn't one on the island already, it'll take forever to get here." Faye breathed through pursed lips. "I'm scared about the baby."

"Shh. It's going to be all right. Babies are well insulated." Hazel had no idea how bad the fall had been, but a red bruise was quickly spreading on Faye's forehead.

She squeezed Faye's hand, her own fingers trembling. "I can borrow my neighbor's car. I'll call the hospital but tell them I'll drive you myself, okay? It will be faster."

"Okay," Faye swallowed. "Do it quickly, please."

"Do you have cramps? Anything like that?"

Faye closed her eyes, checking in with herself. "No cramping," she reported. "I think. But it hurts right here." She pointed to her left side.

"I'll let them know." Hazel helped Faye up so she could sit on the bench.

"I'm cold."

Hazel ran into the back to grab her phone and a wool blanket. She spread it over her fallen bride, who wore nothing but a silk slip. "Here."

"Thanks." Faye pulled the blanket around herself. "Can you call?"

"Yes." Hazel picked up the phone to dial when the wedding bell over the door rang again.

"Hello? Anybody in?"

"Shoot," Hazel whispered. "Give me one second to lock the door, Faye." Pressing the phone to her ear, she hurried to the front. "Sorry, the store is closed."

A man in his twenties frowned at her. "But the door is open. I came to talk about a dress you refused to sell my mother last week."

Jenny had a son? "I'm sorry, I was... We just had an accident in the dressing room. I need to go to the hospital right now." Hazel shook her phone as if that would help fix the bad reception, feeling like she was going to cry any second.

"What sort of accident?" The man was already striding toward her, the frown gone, his gaze focused. "What happened? I'm a doctor. Are you all right?"

"It's not me. My customer fell down and hurt herself." Hazel turned, waving him to come. "Back here. She's pregnant."

"River, is that you?" Faye called out. Clearly, she had recognized his voice. "I stumbled and fell on my belly. My ankle hurts; I can't walk. Can you help me?"

"Faye?" River ran the last few steps to his mother's friend and bent over her, taking her hand. "What hurts exactly? Show me."

"Mostly my head and my ankle. But I don't care about them. I'm worried about the baby. I wasn't able to break my fall."

"*I* care," River murmured and gave the growing bruise on Faye's temple a critical look. "You hit your belly?" He lifted the blanket where it covered Faye's ankle and shook his head.

"I fell right on it."

"No sharp edge dug into your belly, though? No bleeding or contractions? May I?" He put a hand on Faye's belly.

"I don't think so."

The fear in Faye's voice made Hazel dial the hospital again, but again, her cell phone didn't have reception. "I'm going to run outside to call the hospital," she called, holding up her phone as an explanation.

For the first time, River smiled. "I have service," he said and pulled out his own phone. "But you can always dial 911, even if you have no service. They just won't be able to call you back in case you get interrupted."

"Oh." Hazel exhaled, glad he was taking over. "I didn't know."

River dialed and exchanged a few quick words before ending the call. "Okay." He sounded reassuringly calm. "I can feel Baby kick. We'll be all right."

Faye visibly relaxed. "Are you sure?"

He smiled. "They'll be ready to do an ultrasound, but babies are well protected. Let me see your eyes."

"My eyes?"

"We don't want a concussion." He pulled a skinny flashlight from his jacket pocket. "Can you look up for me? Follow the light with your eyes. Okay. Good. Pupils look good, Faye. I'd say you have a nasty bruise and a sprained ankle." He took her wrist and glanced at his watch. "Your pulse is a bit quick, but it's already slowing down again." He nodded and put the light back. "How are you feeling now?"

"My ankle still hurts, but never mind that." A faint hue returned to Faye's pale cheeks. "I'm just worried about the baby."

"Well, sounds like an ultrasound and an ice pack are just the thing, then." River rose and looked at Hazel. "Would you be able to dress her if she sits on the chair?"

"Of course." Hazel nodded, glad to have a task.

River put a hand on her shoulder, and the focused look returned to his blue eyes. "Are you okay? A little shocked yourself, maybe?"

"You could say that," she whispered. Now that any immediate danger to mom and baby seemed over, Hazel's throat constricted. She should have stayed to help. Even if the baby was perfectly fine—what if Faye sued her? Thoughts of liability rose in the back of Hazel's mind, ready to blossom and multiply the moment she'd be alone.

Without further ado, River took her wrist and felt her pulse. Hazel focused on his touch to squelch her rising fears. His fingers felt warm and sure.

"Mmh." He let go and turned away to put the fallen curtain rod back in the brackets. "My car is not far away. I'm going to bring it to the door."

"You can't drive on Lover's Lane," Hazel said. "The closest we can get is the small parking lot across the bridge. We'll have to support Faye to get over there."

"I can carry her. Are you okay with that, Faye?"

"I am if you are."

"All right." River gave Faye a last glance before he nodded at Hazel and lowered the curtain. The sound of his steps quickly receded.

Hazel picked Faye's maternity dress from the floor. "I'm going to pull it over your head, okay? I'll be as gentle as I can." She took care to stay clear of the bruise.

"I'm sorry, Hazel," Faye said when she slipped her arms into the sleeves. "I should've accepted your help when you offered it."

"It was an accident. It's not like you planned to fall and hurt yourself."

"Still." With a groan, Faye turned sideways so Hazel could zip the dress. "Thanks. At least I'm decent now." She sighed and slumped back. "Oh, the shame. I was lying there like a fat beetle in underwear..."

That made Hazel smile. "You were wearing a pretty silk slip. I promise neither River nor I saw any underwear."

"Ha-ha." Faye said the words, not believing Hazel, but then she chuckled at herself. "Thanks for trying. I guess it'll turn into a story to tell. As long as the baby is okay."

That made Hazel's mouth go dry again. "Just sit quietly until he brings the car." She tried to swallow. "Is his full name River Summers?"

Faye put her hands on her belly. "Yes, it is. He's Jenny's son."

"I think he came to tell me off about the dress." Hazel slid down onto the floor beside Faye's bench. Now that the adrenaline was leaving her, she felt like crying. With a sigh, Hazel buried her head in her hands.

A hand touched her shoulder. "I'll tell him to take it easy on you," Faye promised. "Don't worry about it."

"Thanks." With a wan smile, Hazel looked up. "Things aren't going great lately."

Faye squeezed Hazel's shoulder and shifted position with a wince. "I don't mind telling you, though—I'm glad River came when he did. I feel a lot better now that he talked me down."

"Same." Hazel leaned her head back to rest it against the wall of the changing room. Even if he was mad at her, she was glad River had come when he did too.

In fact, Hazel couldn't wait for River to come back. When she finally heard the bell ring and his long strides crossing the room, Hazel closed her eyes and took a long, deep, silent breath of relief.

CHAPTER 8
The Past

I thought it would be different." Marianne lifted her arms, and her mother cinched the waist. "Oof. Too tight. I can't breathe, Mama. They tie them loose now."

"None of us can breathe, darling." Mama loosened the corset a little before tying the knot. "How did you think it would be different, Marianne? Did you think it would be more romantic?"

"Yes, for one." Marianne bit her lip to suppress the thought of Robert's eyes gliding over her like cold hands, lingering in all the wrong places. She pulled on her blouse and skirt.

Mama started to close the buttons on the back. "That's only in the novels I keep telling you not to read." Her voice was soft, as if she didn't quite believe that herself.

"But you and Papa seem all right." Marianne glanced over her shoulder.

"Marriage is not like dime novel writers make it out to be," Mama insisted.

But Marianne caught her mother's worried look.

So romance *was* like dime novel writers said—just not for her and Robert. She turned back to the mirror. A frown crimped her forehead.

Mama cleared her throat. "But you always liked him, Marianne. It must be just nerves."

"He's different now that we are engaged."

"How is he different?" Her mother's face appeared beside Marianne's reflection.

"He acts as if I belong to him. It makes me feel like I'm a doll, not a person." Marianne turned, letting the skirt swing. "It's so long. I won't be able to climb."

"You're not *supposed* to climb those dreadful cliffs. I've told you a million times."

Marianne opened her hands in question. "What am I to do, Mama? Sit around and pretend I'm a doll for Robert's benefit?" She snorted.

"Marianne!"

"Mama, you don't hear him talk the way he does when he and I are alone. Robert does what he wants."

"He has a business to run and important decisions to make. Of course he does what he wants. He must stand on his own two feet. Klara is a seamstress. She won't be able to help him out if... But she says he's doing very well."

Marianne wasn't so sure. People never mentioned getting their lumber at Robert's mill. The wood was too expensive, and the quality was not as good as what the Donovans offered. More than once, Robert had mentioned that Marianne's dowry would fix things and set him up.

Marianne had no plans of pouring her money into the sawmill. But as she understood it, she would not have much choice in the matter.

She put her hands on her waist. "I must stand on my own two feet too. Why should I not do what I like?" she said rebelliously. "I *like* stones and fossils. In fact, it's the only thing I like anymore. And I haven't read a novel in... I don't know. In a long time. I read only scientific books now."

"If you won't save my poor nerves, at least make sure Robert doesn't mind your talking," Mama murmured. "He likes to keep up appearances, and Klara thinks it's important for his business. I'm sure he doesn't want his fiancée to climb across cliffs like a rock crab."

That made Marianne laugh. "I'm not a *rock crab*, Mama. I'm actually very graceful. And I find the most incredible fossils. I even wrote about the last one to a professor at the university."

"What professor?"

"A Professor Whitman. Papa said he was young but very bright and with a shining career ahead of him."

"Stop writing letters to strangers, child." But Mama smiled indulgently. "You and your fossils. You won't have time for them once you have a family. Did you at least show Papa the letter before you posted it?"

"Yes, and he said it was good. I included a drawing of my latest find."

"Did you now?" Mama tried to hide her face, bustling to the dresser, but Marianne could hear the note of pride swinging in it. Mama loved her drawings and had hung many of them in frames around the house.

"Yep." Marianne lifted the hem of her skirt and sighed. It was a pity she wasn't allowed to wear trousers.

And it was more than a pity that Robert should be able to prevent her from hunting fossils.

She had secretly pictured herself showing him her best spots, maybe taking a picnic and making it a romantic outing. She had thought she could happily merge her old life with the new.

But what if Robert found her ideas of hunting fossils would damage his appearance? There would be no more secret slipping away to walk on windblown bluffs and digging for the petrified remains of ammonites and algae and fish.

What if Marianne lost interest in always sitting home? What if she didn't like to spend all her time with babies?

Did that ever happen to a woman?

"Here." Mama had returned from the dresser. "I made you this to hold up the skirt on your walks. Mind you, it's only for when you are on your own. *Please* don't use it in town."

Marianne's eyes widened. "How beautiful, Mama!"

"I had the goldsmith make an ammonite pin for your dress. I attached a loop to it, and when you do like this..." Mama deftly needled the large pin through the gathered fabric of the skirt. Then she wound the pin's elastic loop through Marianne's belt and snapped it back over the pin to lift the skirt. "Voilà. You can make it as short or as long as you like now. No more clutching your skirt in dirty hands and leaving muddy wrinkles. When you get back to civilization, just open the pin and let the skirt down, clean and wrinkle-free."

Delighted, Marianne clasped her hands. "Mama, I *love* it! It's the most thoughtful gift! Mama!" She slung her arms around her mother and hugged her tight, deeply inhaling her comforting, familiar scent of freshly baked bread and lavender. "Oh, I wish I could just stay with you and Papa forever. I love you so much."

Her mother cleared her throat before she answered. "I love you so much too, my darling," she said then and patted Marianne's back. "But what nonsense to want to stay with Papa and me. Don't you want children? And with all your stubbornness, you'll love having your own house. You always said you would."

"Um." Marianne sighed and released her mother. "Robert is too... He really isn't who I thought he was."

Frowning, Mama touched the pin. "You knew Robert would ask you to marry him. You wanted him to do it."

"I did." Maybe they hadn't met often enough, especially in the last few years when they both had grown into adults.

Robert had been busy with studies and traveling and setting up his business. And Marianne, content to follow her own interests, had dreamed more about her future than taking pains to visit Robert when he was home. Now, she regretted her lax attitude. She needed advice. "Mama? I find Robert's company stifling."

Mam looked up. "Stifling?"

"Yes. I don't know what to say when he is around. Every time we take a walk, I find myself wishing it would be shorter. And I only suggest the shortest paths I can think of." She cleared her throat, embarrassed at being so bad at romance. "And even then, I wish they were still a lot shorter."

Mama started to fold the nightgown Marianne had tossed on the bed. "It takes time. What do you talk about on your walks?"

Marianne shrugged. "He talks about his business, and his time at the university—what pranks he played on his professors and how good his grades were, nonetheless. There is not usually any time for me to talk, which is just as well since I wouldn't know what to say to him."

She didn't fancy herself in love with Mateo, the boy she had kissed two years ago. Their lives had been too different.

But she remembered very well the way they had talked by the fire. Never for a moment did they run out of things to say, even though the only thing they had in common was a grilled fish and a beach bonfire and a single sweet and salty kiss.

Shouldn't it be that much easier to talk with Robert, whom she'd known all her life?

"You never say anything at all?" Mama asked, sounding surprised.

"Sometimes I have to fill an awkward moment," Marianne admitted.

"Do you bore him with your stones and sediments?"

Marianne straightened her shoulders. "No, I do not, Mama. I'll turn nineteen in three weeks and know better than to tell Robert about stones. It's just a matter of time until he returns to talking about himself."

Mama sighed. "Oh well, these young men... I suppose he is used to the company of other young fellows and his business partners. That would teach any man to talk about himself. You'll have to guide him into being more considerate in his conversation. Just don't hurt his pride. They don't like that."

"No danger there," Marianne muttered, but she'd turned away and luckily, Mama didn't hear. "May I take a walk to try my new pin while you and Grandmama visit the neighbors?"

"You don't want to come?" Mama's face fell with disappointment.

"I've been sitting around all day. My legs are starting to twitch."

"Goodness. Stop mentioning twitching legs, child. You're not a spider." Mama straightened her back. "Your grandmother will miss you."

"She's probably on her ship, smearing tar on the rudder and planning excuses to skip the neighbors herself." Marianne ducked out of the way, laughing, when her mother tried to swat her bottom for her impudence.

Grandmama Phoebe would be the first to understand why Marianne preferred to climb cliffs and scrape barnacles rather than sit in stuffy drawing rooms, bored and sipping enough tea to drown a pufferfish.

"Enjoy yourself, and tell Grandmama I will scrape the barnacles off the rowboat so she doesn't have to." Too agile to be caught, Marianne leaned in and planted a kiss on her mother's cheek, then skipped out of the room in her new, pinned, practical dress.

CHAPTER 9

Hazel? Did I get the name right?"

Hazel put the can of kidney beans back on the shelf and turned. "Hi." She smiled at the young woman who had come up to her. "Yes, you did. I'm Hazel."

"I'm Zoe." She held out a hand, and Hazel shook it. "I'm sorry for bothering you," Zoe said. "I realize you don't know me. I'm visiting my parents who live in the cove, and my mom bought the dress for her recommitment ceremony at your store."

"Oh, yes! Hi, Zoe. Nice to meet you."

"I recognized you from my mom's description and thought I'd introduce myself." Zoe checked over her shoulder to make sure she wasn't blocking the narrow aisle and pushed her shopping cart to the side. "There are so few young people in the cove. It's nice to see someone my own age."

"I know what you mean. Most of my friends from school have left for college or jobs in bigger towns." Hazel smiled, glad Zoe didn't want to talk about the wedding dress mix-up. Or Faye's fall.

"I've only been to the island a handful of times," Zoe confided. "But I saw a couple of cute cafés sprinkled around the harbor. Would you like to grab a coffee by any chance?"

"Sure." Involuntarily, Hazel glanced at her own empty cart.

"Unless you are busy," Zoe said quickly. "No worries."

"Not really." Hazel could buy groceries the next day. "Should we leave right now? I still have another half hour on my lunch break."

"Let me tell my friend Audrey so she can join us. You'll like her. We came over to the island together, and she'll want to meet you too." Zoe smiled, already tapping on her phone to text her friend as they pushed the carts to the exit. "She'll meet us at the café," Zoe reported and tucked the phone back into her jeans pocket. "I was going to get some snacks, but coffee and cake sounds so much better. My treat, by the way."

"That's not necessary," Hazel protested as they left the market, stepping into the sunshine.

"I'm not going to randomly pick up girls in the store and make them buy pastries." Zoe unceremoniously slipped her arm under Hazel's.

Hazel smiled. "All right then," she agreed. "This random girl says thank you."

Zoe laughed and started walking toward the harbor while she talked about how much she'd enjoyed the ferry ride from the cove. Eventually, she mentioned Faye's fall. "Was it bad?"

"It was," Hazel said weakly. "It happened two days ago, and my knees still get soft when I think about it. I called to ask how she is, but she didn't pick up. I didn't want to leave a message."

"I bet your life flashed in front of your eyes," Zoe said with sympathy in her voice. "I work in a bakery. I know what it means for a small business when an accident like that happens."

Hazel stopped walking and braced herself. She needed to know what had happened. "Do you know how she is? Is the baby okay?"

Zoe turned to her, surprise in her eyes. "The baby is perfectly fine," she said. "Faye has a sprained ankle and a small bump on her head, but she's hopping around on a crutch and laughs about how clumsy she's becoming. Did nobody let you know?"

Suddenly dizzy, Hazel took a few steadying breaths. Then she shook her head. "No, I didn't know. But I'm so glad."

"You poor thing," Zoe murmured and patted Hazel's back. "I'm sorry you were left hanging. Everyone's fine. Relieved?"

"Yeah. Thank you for telling me." She straightened again. "Is Faye angry with me?"

Zoe's eyebrows rose in surprise. "I don't know why she would be? She keeps telling everyone and their uncle that it was her own fault for thinking she could still balance on one foot."

Hazel exhaled. "I feel so much better." They started walking again, following the sandy, meandering lane leading down to the harbor. Already the ocean spread before them, glittering in the October sun. The salty breeze tousled Hazel's and Zoe's long hair and dotted the sea's rippling waves with white foam. A line of pelicans flew, long and low, toward the cliffs.

Hazel tucked a flying strand of hair behind her ear. "Um...your friend Audrey?"

"Hmm? What about her?" They reached the end of the lane, and Zoe started climbing down the stairs leading to the small restaurants and coffee places that lined the quay.

"Is she from Mendocino Cove too?" Hazel tried to sound casual. But she wanted to be forewarned. It was starting to feel as if all young people lately were somehow related to the wedding dress debacle.

Zoe smiled as if she knew what Hazel was really asking. "Yes, she is. Actually, she's Jenny's daughter. Audrey is going to run the old hotel at Beach and Forgotten."

"I see." So Audrey and River were siblings. "Are you sure Audrey wants to meet me?"

"Sure." Zoe stopped. "Why not?"

"Have you heard about Jenny's dress?"

"The one you wouldn't sell her." Zoe nodded. "Faye said you had to promise *never* to sell any dresses to her family so you could inherit the store."

Hazel nodded. "What makes it worse is that it really *was* Jenny's perfect dress. Audrey and River should be angry with me."

Zoe tilted her head. "Audrey just inherited a hotel. I'm sure she would have promised a whole lot of things too, if her mom had asked." She suddenly raised her arm and waved. "That's her right there."

A few hundred yards away, another young woman raised a hand to wave back.

CHAPTER 10

They reached Audrey, and Hazel introduced herself. Audrey already knew who she was, and when Hazel apologized one more time about Jenny's dress, Audrey shook her head, smiled, and said it was no big deal.

"Let's go to the new café over there." Zoe pointed. "I've been meaning to try it out for a while."

Audrey laughed as they started toward it. "It's hardly new. It's been there for at least six months."

"That's brand-spanking new for this island," Hazel said and smiled. "Most businesses here have been around for ages."

Zoe opened the door to the café, and they filed inside.

Hazel smoothed her windblown hair as she followed Audrey to a window table. It was a pretty place full of light and wood and gleaming brass. And yet, they were the only customers.

"Hi." The barista, leaning on the coffee machine, looked up from her phone and grinned. "Windy outside?"

"A little bit." Audrey also raked back her hair as she sat.

The barista, who was maybe ten or so years older than themselves and had a bright red mane, crossed her tattooed arms. "What can I get you three honey buns?"

Zoe looked around their group. "Anything you like, ladies."

Audrey glanced at Hazel, who quickly shrugged. "Whatever sounds good to you. I'm not particular." She was hungry, but she didn't mind. She didn't want Zoe and Audrey to think that she was taking advantage of the situation.

Audrey picked a folded menu card from the small stand on the table and opened it, positioning it so Hazel could see as well. "Zoe, I might need more than a piece of cake." Hazel caught the look that went between the two friends.

"Sure." Zoe smiled brightly. "I got you."

Hazel looked down at the card again, her eyes scanning the lines of print without taking them in.

It would be nice to have a friend who understood glances and hints.

Most of Hazel's friends from school had left the island. There weren't enough jobs for young people, and most wandered off in pursuit of their careers. The ones who stayed were married and busy with husbands and kids. Hazel saw them once in a while. But the old connection was gone, and while Hazel tried to still be a good friend, sooner or later the conversation turned to experiences she couldn't share. Hazel was married only to a failing business.

"Hazel? Do you want to share a strawberry cheese-cake crepe with me?" Audrey flipped through the menu. "Or a savory one? Ham and gruyère? What do you feel like?"

Hazel looked up, surprised. Like Zoe, Audrey treated her as if they'd known each other for years. "I'd love to share something."

Satisfied, Audrey nodded. "Help me out. I can't decide which one."

"Um. Cheesecake?"

"Perfect."

"Got something in mind?" The barista pulled out her pad and slapped it on the counter. Clearly, she wasn't going to the trouble of coming over.

Zoe grinned. "Is this your café?" she asked. "It's beautiful."

"Yep." The barista grinned back. "Do you want it? I'll sell it to you. I can't *wait* to get back to New York. I've had my fix of the simple life, and my dad said he'd buy me an espresso bar in Brooklyn if I want out." She lowered her voice. "You're the first people to come in here today. I'm bored out of my skull. I do want out. Believe me."

"Wish I could." Zoe sighed. "Actually, I'm a baker, and I'd love to open a bakery here. But I would barely be able to afford a studio apartment in the cove. I just checked out a couple of them this morning. There's no way I can rent this place."

"Who said anything about renting? Not me." The barista scribbled something on her pad and ripped off the page, then folded it into an airplane and shot it in Zoe's direction. "Here's my number if you want to talk. I haven't got a clue how much Dad wants to sell for, but I could picture myself putting in a word or twenty for you. Anything to get me out." She winked. "He's no pushover, but his time is too valuable to argue with me."

"Really?" Zoe bent down to pick up the paper airplane that had landed a few inches from her sandal. She unfolded the plane. "I might call you. Don't expect me to jump on anything, though. Like I said, I don't exactly have a ton of savings."

"Maybe your parents will help you out too," the barista decided. "Now, what do you all want? I make a mean flat white."

They named their hot drinks. Zoe asked for a slice of cannelloni torte, and Audrey ordered the strawberry cheesecake crepe.

"Anything else?" The barista was already pulling coffee cups as big as bowls from the shelf.

"Uh, we'll also take a ham and gruyère crepe. Sorry, Zo." Audrey grinned at her friend. "I'll buy next time."

"Oh, is that what we're doing, eating whatever we want? Fine." Zoe pointed at the display case. "Then I'll also have a slice of Schwartzwalder torte."

"Good choice." The barista nodded contentedly. Humming a tune under her breath, she set about preparing the orders. It didn't take long for the crepes and roasted beans to fill the air with a delicious, rich, seductive aroma.

Hazel pressed a hand to her stomach to keep it from growling.

Soon they had coffee bowls topped high with foamed milk and powdered with cinnamon, hot crepes, and cream cakes in front of them.

Audrey cut both crepes and put the two bigger pieces on the plate she pushed over to Hazel.

"That's too much," Hazel protested. "You didn't share it evenly."

"I couldn't button my jeans this morning. This will have to do for me," Audrey announced. "Between Jon's cooking and Hannah's food truck and Billie's breakfasts, I'm in trouble. You, on the other hand... Of course you look fantastic, but I was a bit worried the wind would blow you into the water."

"Hmm." Defensively, Hazel crossed her arms over her chest.

"Audrey, don't comment on the way people look," Zoe grumbled.

"You're right. Sorry, Hazel," Audrey said immediately. "I didn't really think the wind would blow you in the water. I'm just jealous. I wish I was that skinny. I apologize."

"No—it's okay." Warmth shot up Hazel's neck, but she smiled. She'd been teased as a kid for being too skinny, and the apology felt nice. She tried a corner of the cheesecake crepe and leaned back, chewing with her eyes closed. "Mh-hmm. This is *so* good."

"Do you bake everything yourself?" Zoe asked the Brooklyn barista.

"I have it delivered. I was getting around to baking, but I lost steam somewhere in the middle. Right after ordering the equipment, to be exact. Poor Dad." She sighed. "Turns out hot coffee drinks are my true passion. Who would have thought, huh? I'd hoped it would be music or art or anything. But no, it has to be the perfect cappuccino. Oh well."

Zoe smiled. "How were you going to do the baking?"

The barista pointed over her shoulder. "I started to remodel the back. If baking is your thing, you're in luck. The ovens and things aren't hooked up yet, but they're there. I ordered good appliances because Dad said not to skimp on the wrong end. I'll throw everything in if you want to take over, because honestly? I'm not going to schlepp stand mixers I don't plan on using across the country."

"Sounds perfect, and also very expensive. But I would love to have a look."

"Now?"

"If you don't mind."

"Sure. Come on." The barista waved Zoe over, and the two disappeared.

Audrey set down her fork. "I'm full," she said, regret swinging in her voice. "It's like my mom's breakfasts. All her friends come over, and everyone brings tons of food. You have to see it to believe it. Or better yet, join me for one."

"I doubt your mom and her friends want to see me," Hazel said, covering her mouth with her hand because she was still chewing.

"Believe me, Mom would love to see you. She's always on my case about making friends. Zoe is in Seattle most of the time. Since Mom is building a new house with her fiancé, I'll soon be stuck with only my great-aunt for company." She took a sip of her coffee. "Who's *fabulous*. But it's not the same as having friends, if you know what I mean."

Hazel nodded. "I do know what you mean." She finally set down her fork. The rich food and warm drink suffused her with a cozy, content feeling. Life seemed so much easier with friendship. "If you're serious, I'll come visit you sometime. I haven't left the island in weeks. And I've never been to the forgotten cove myself. I'd love to see it."

"I'm serious," was all Audrey had time to say before Zoe, her eyes round, joined them again.

"Goodness," she whispered as she sat down. "It's a total dream back there."

"Did she say more about the price? She must have *some* idea," Audrey whispered back. "Is it doable?"

Zoe shook her head. "It can't be cheap," she murmured. "Only the best brand names and everything new."

"You could ask if she would consider a profit share arrangement," Hazel said softly. "With an option to buy her out when the time comes."

"Is that possible?" Zoe propped her chin on her hand. "Maybe I will."

"Hey, girly? Call me for sure." The Brooklyn barista reappeared behind the counter, drying her hands on a kitchen towel. "I'll ask Dad to give me some numbers."

Zoe nodded and looked at her cake. "It's really good, but I can't eat now. All that excitement cost me my appetite."

"You know what? Talking about selling this place has done me good. I feel like I just flipped a new page. I have to get outside." The barista put her hands on her hips. "I'll close down for the week and go see my friend in San Francisco. Right now. Do you guys want to take home the rest of all the cakes and fruit I have?"

Zoe laughed. "You really don't care about the bottom line, do you?"

The barista grinned. "Never had to, lucky little me. By some random stroke of luck, I get to only care about experiences. And right now, I want to experience a sourdough bowl with hot clam chowder on Fisherman's Wharf. So you want free cake or nah?"

"Hazel?" Zoe smiled at her. "Instead of going shopping?"

Hazel smiled back. "Sure."

"Finally. Thank you. Give me a moment to pack things up."

Half an hour later, Hazel stepped out of the store, carrying bags full of cream cakes to brighten her afternoon. The wind had died down, and the Pacific Ocean lay like a breathing, shimmering pearl in the harbor.

"Audrey, we should catch that ferry," Zoe said after checking the time on her cell phone. They hurried to the dock, where it smelled of diesel and saltwater, sun-warm metal and black mussels. Screaming gulls circled the big boat as it waited for its passengers, swooping on the ice cream cones and hot dogs of innocent pedestrians. Audrey and Zoe hurried to get on while Hazel waited to wave goodbye to her new friends.

The attendant pushed the gangway in. Zoe was already climbing the metal stairs to the upper deck, but Audrey stopped at the bottom rung. "Hazel?"

"Yes?" Hazel shaded her eyes against the light reflecting off the glittering ocean.

"My brother, River? He said he *likes* you."

"He *likes* me?" Hazel felt a warmth spread to her cheeks that had nothing to do with friendship or cherry cream. "I thought he was angry over the dress."

"Maybe he was before he met you. I don't think he is anymore," Audrey called out. "And now that I've met you, I think I know why."

Grinning, the attendant locked the gangway door, and the ferry's engine rumbled to life.

"Then tell River hi from me," Hazel called back over the noise. "Tell him thanks very much for helping Faye."

Audrey smiled as the ferry pushed off. "Anything else I should tell him?"

Hazel couldn't think, but then, at the last minute before the ferry steered into the ocean, she held up her bags and yelled, "Tell him to visit if he likes cannelloni cake!"

Laughing, Audrey waved. "He *adores* cannelloni! Though I don't think he needs another reason to visit. See you soon!"

The ferry turned, whisking Zoe and Audrey out of sight.

"See you soon," Hazel said softly. Then she held her face up to the sky. "Mom? Did you hear that?"

Only a breeze whispered back, caressing Hazel's cheeks the way her mother's hand used to do. Hazel closed her eyes, savoring the light touch until it was gone. Then she picked up her paper bags full of silky cream, decadent chocolate, and melt-in-the-mouth sponge cake and walked back to her little store on Lover's Lane.

Everyone in the Summers family seemed so nice. What could have caused a family feud bad enough to tie the store's inheritance to such a hostile promise?

Hazel let herself in and ran upstairs to put the cake into her fridge. It barely fit, but she managed to wedge the boxes and cartons just so. Then she washed her hands and went into the living room. When she walked past the family's old applewood secretary desk, she paused to look at it. She never used it anymore because it was crammed full of the papers, pins, and pencils of generations. Every time she opened it, something fell out.

Sometime soon, Hazel would have to clean up that mess the past had left behind.

CHAPTER 11
The Past

I t's not enough, and you know it." Smiling her most charming smile, Marianne pushed the small stack of coins back across the counter.

Henry, the old bookseller, leaned forward. "It won't come out in one piece. Maybe it's not even a fish."

"Oh, it's a fish. Here, what do you think that is?" She pointed at the obvious. "The tail fin is half exposed where the slate fell off. The rest is intact, hidden in the rock. Whether it comes out in one piece depends only on your skill."

Henry squinted at the fossilized fin. "Fine. It's a fish," he admitted.

"The slate is ready to crack open on its own. All it needs is a little tap. But if you think it's too hard... Sure." Marianne shrugged. The golden light of a fine day was fading, and she had to rush home to change before dinner. If Robert saw her like this, he would have one of his silent fits and not talk for an entire hour.

"I'd better send it to the museum," she said and slowly opened her padded knapsack to stow her prize away.

"Wait—wait."

Marianne smiled to herself. She'd recognized the light in Henry's eyes when she first pulled out the fossil. He couldn't help himself any more than she could. After all, he'd taught her almost everything she knew about fossils. Where to find them, how to dig them out, the best way of removing their ancient rock shells.

Now that he was too old to hunt himself, her finds were the only thing to bring that light back.

"I'll tell you what," she said graciously. "I'll trade. I don't even need money."

"I should think not," he murmured. "But I don't suppose you'll let me have him for free. So, what do you have in mind?"

Marianne glanced out the shop window to make sure no other customers were in sight and then, unladylike, propped an elbow on the counter. "I want to have the first pick from the box of books standing over there."

Henry's furtive glance told her it was a worthy demand. "Nah," he tried to play it off. "That's just old stuff from the Widow Smith."

"Yes, I know it is." She grinned and hovered a hand on the fossil as if she were getting ready to pull it back into her open knapsack. "One single pick, and you get the fish. Deal?"

"Oh...oh all right. You drive a hard bargain, young lady."

"I learned from the best." She winked cheekily.

Finally, the old man cracked a smile. "You sure know how to flatter me. Go ahead and open the box then."

Eagerly, he reached for the fossil to inspect it under a lamp.

The sky was turning the deep, velvety blue of a summer plum already. Marianne knew she would have to run most of the way to the cove, hoping nobody would spot her and tattle to Mama. Or Robert. Or Klara.

She pried open the box and spread her skirt to kneel on the sun-warm wood floor. Quickly, her fingers riffled through the contents, checking through books and unbound manuscripts. It had been months since she last got her hands on a scientific paper, and her brain was starved for more.

But there was nothing like that here, nothing relevant to science at all. It appeared that the Widow Smith had hidden less in her library than Marianne hoped. She rocked back on her heels because now, she truly was out of time.

"I'll just take this." She grabbed a roll of yellowing paper with crumbling edges. At least it was old.

Henry looked up and popped the watchmaker's magnifying glass off his eye. "What is it?"

"I don't know." Marianne rose and smoothed her skirt. She was grateful for the big pin Mama had given her. She needed to run fast, and it would be easier without fabric flapping about her ankles and making her stumble on every other stride.

"Well, open it." Henry peered over the counter.

"I have to get home. I'll open it when you open the rock. I suppose we both can look forward to a surprise."

His eyes smiled, and he nodded because, despite all his grumpiness, old Henry was the sweetest man alive. "I hope it turns out good for both of us. Tell me what your price is next time you stop by."

"I will. Goodbye!" Marianne tucked her rolled-up prize into her knapsack, threw it over her shoulder, and left the store. She walked as fast as she could until she left Main Street and stepped onto the sandy path that led through the wildflowers on the bluff toward the cliffs lining the cove. She peered over her shoulder. There was not a person in sight. Everybody was home, either dressing for dinner or dressing up their dinner, depending on their circumstance.

Pressing her bag tight so it wouldn't bounce and crumble her new possession, Marianne started to run.

She was a good runner, with long, strong legs that were fit from climbing. Best of all, she loved the exhilaration of running, the way it felt to fly, light-footed, across the bluff over the ocean, as free as a gull.

She tiptoed into the house and made it up the stairs without seeing anyone. In her room, she quickly washed her face and arms, unpinned her sandy, muddy skirt, and tossed it on a chair to brush out later. Then she slipped into a morning gown, pulled the cream-colored dress from her closet and laid it on the bed, fastened a strand of pearls around her neck, hastily pinned her messy hair up in a way Mama would probably want to talk about later, and checked her pocket watch.

A light knock told her that she had done well. She took a quick breath, hoping her cheeks were not flaming red from rushing around. "Come in, Tessie."

Tessie stepped into the room and closed the door. "I'm here to help you with your hair." Smiling at Marianne's state, she shook her head. "Just got home, huh? What are you going to wear?"

"I thought I'd wear that there." Marianne pointed to the dress on the bed.

"We'll need to... Are you even *wearing* a corset? I know they've become shockingly loose, but the dress won't fit around *that* waist. Sheesh."

"It's a new time, Tessie. Soon, women will wear trousers and no corset at all! I've already seen them do it when I went to San Francisco with Papa."

"Well, sugar plum, you wear trousers when your mama says you may and not a day before." Tessie's experienced fingers loosened the strings and retied them before she helped Marianne into the dress. While she busied herself with the ridiculously long row of tiny buttons in the back, Marianne grabbed her knapsack and pulled out the roll of yellowing paper.

"Ooh," Tessie said indulgently. "What have you dragged back now?"

"Henry traded it for a fish. I don't know what it is. I didn't have time to check it." Gently, Marianne unrolled the paper.

"Be careful," Tessie scolded. "The paper is crumbling all over the place. What a mess!"

Marianne frowned at the scattered bits on the rug. "It's really old," she murmured. "It seems to be a map. Don't you agree?"

Tessie slipped the last button through its hole and straightened, looking over Marianne's shoulder as she started pulling the pins from her hair. "Yes, it does seem to be an old map. It looks perfectly useless, in my opinion—don't use it to find your way to the market." She pointed. "Look how short Main Street was. It is much longer now. You'll lose yourself if you follow this. Where is your brush?"

"On the dresser," Marianne murmured, not taking her eyes off the map. "You're right, that must be Main. I wonder...hmm."

"Maybe it's from the fellow who ran away to join that French pirate in Monterey," Tessie said comfortably. She had fetched the brush and pressed Marianne into a chair to do her hair. "It happened a long time ago. But the legend has it he came back and hid his treasure in the cove for safekeeping." It was one of Tessie's favorite town stories, and she used to tell it to Marianne at bedtime.

"You're right. Maybe it is. Finally proof positive that it is true." Marianne smiled. "Ouch. Careful with the pins, if you don't mind." She rubbed her scalp.

Marianne knew full well Tessie was only making a joke. But the family in question insisted that the old story was true, and if a treasure ever *were* to be found, it should be theirs.

Almost everyone in town had searched for it as a kid. Without success, naturally. But Marianne didn't think someone who had worked for an infamous pirate would hide their treasure where kids could find it.

She turned the scroll in her hands and squinted. "If it's a treasure map, then where's the treasure?"

Tessie gave the map another casual glance. "Well, *there*. Turn the map back around, silly. See the mark there? That would be it, wouldn't it?"

"Oh." Now Marianne, too, started to make sense of the squiggly lines and marks. "Yes, you must be right. Where did you learn to read maps like that, Tessie?"

"My brother is a sailor," she replied cheerfully. "My father was a sailor, and even my grandfather was a sailor. Maps and ships and cliffs and currents are all they talk about. If you ever want to get a word in at the dinner table, you'd better know a thing or two about it all."

"I'd have never made it out myself."

"My father always said I had a talent in that quarter." Tessie put the last pin in place. "I reckon maybe I do."

"You are marvelous." Marianne jumped up and kissed Tessie on the cheek.

"Does your mama know about the map?" Tessie asked casually, pulling the loose strands from the brush to toss them.

"Um. Not yet."

"Yes, I see. Well, you might mention it to her tonight. Do you hear? I won't stand by and watch you get lost following some nonsense map old Henry gave you."

"I'm almost nineteen," Marianne protested weakly. "When's a girl finally allowed to do what she wants?"

"When she turns fifty, like me. Do as I say, please."

"Yes, Tessie. I will tell everyone about the map at the dinner table." Marianne sighed. She was not looking forward to it. Their family dinners were usually comfortable, merry affairs. But with Klara and Robert joining them, it would be different. "Have Grandmama and Grandpa returned from their boating trip yet?" she asked, groping for a spark of hope.

"I haven't seen them. Don't count on their company."

Suddenly feeling fatigued, Marianne frowned.

Tessie sighed. "Cheer up, sugar plum. Who knows? Maybe Robert is interested in maps, like the men in my family. It could be something to talk about."

"That will be the day," Marianne murmured under her breath, quiet enough that Tessie didn't have to reply.

The last thing Robert would want to talk about was an old treasure map.

CHAPTER 12

Audrey flicked off a crumb of shortcake clinging to her knit sweater and opened the front door. "Hazel! You found the hotel. Well done."

Hazel smiled. "My neighbor dropped me off. We did have to circle back to find Forgotten Lane."

"Oh, I know. It's a real problem. I thought if I just cut back the greenery up there, it'd be easier to see. In fact, it hasn't made a lick of difference." Audrey stepped aside to let Hazel in. Her new acquaintance looked lovely in a lilac-colored cotton dress that was tailored to perfection and darling black kitten heels.

"I brought these for your mom." Hazel showed the bouquet of wildflowers in her hand. "They are California asters and tidy tips from the island."

"She'll love them. But you didn't have to bring anything."

"I wanted to." Hazel came inside, looking around curiously. "What a beautiful house, Audrey. You must enjoy living here."

"I do. I fell for it the moment I saw it. And I'm glad I'll get to share it with guests." Audrey waved to follow her. "Zoe is already here. She's sitting outside with Mom, getting sunburned." She smiled over her shoulder at Hazel. "Zoe isn't used to California's natural wattage." She led her guest through the house and out the open French doors onto the sun-warm patio.

For a moment, Audrey saw the familiar place with fresh eyes: the comfortable wicker chairs and cheerful sun umbrella, the bougainvilleas and ferns in their terracotta pots, the old cypresses shading the sides and the bright beach and sparkling ocean beyond.

"Hey." Zoe smiled a welcome from one of the chairs. She was holding a bowl of strawberries and cream in her hands. The fresh, fruity scent of the berries competed with the fragrance of warm tree resin and the ever-present scent of fresh kelp and salt water.

"Hello, Hazel." Mom looked up. "How are you?"

Audrey heard Hazel release a small, tense breath. "I'm good. How are you?"

Mom smiled. "Great. As well as on my way out. I'd love to spend more time with you all, but work calls." She rose and put down the newspaper she'd been reading. "The university has invited our local high schoolers to have a look around campus. I volunteered to show the history department."

"You are not leaving on my behalf, are you?" Hazel asked. "I really am so sorry about the dress."

Mom had fallen hard for that dress. Luckily, Hazel didn't know her well enough to decipher the small change in the set of her eyebrows and the shape of her mouth.

"Let's forget about that dress once and for all. If you could have sold it to me, you would have." Mom smiled and pointed at the table. "Come and have some strawberries before Audrey shows you around. I bought too many at the market this morning. They are very good, but they won't keep. Everyone has to pitch in." She winked at Hazel, nodded at Zoe, and kissed Audrey on the head. "See you later, darlings."

"Bye, Mom." Audrey waited until Mom had gone inside, then took Hazel's arm and pulled her toward the table. "Here. Sit. I'm going to get fresh cream."

Her new guest protested that it wasn't necessary, but it took Audrey all of thirty seconds to refill the cut-glass bowl in the kitchen before she sat back down at the patio table. "Have some." She pointed but laughed when she saw Zoe's face. "Fine." With a sigh, she fell back into her chair and ran her fingers through her hair. "Fine. I'll stop."

"It's not you, Hazel, it's her. Audrey can't help herself when it comes to feeding people," Zoe explained and set her own empty bowl back on the table. "My theory is that they brainwashed her at hotel college."

"It's not called hotel college." Grinning, Audrey pushed the strawberries closer to Hazel.

"Your mother is still disappointed about the dress, isn't she?" Hazel asked suddenly. "I could tell."

Audrey glanced up, surprised Hazel had noticed after all. "My mother is in the throes of building a house and organizing a wedding and interviewing for a professorship. The dress is the least of her worries."

"Did she find another one yet?" Hazel was single-minded.

"She ordered something online." Audrey had seen Mom's new pick. It was beautiful. The price had struck Audrey as incredibly low for the amount of detail and beading and tailoring shown in the picture. But she'd kept quiet since Mom didn't need any more fuss over her wedding dress.

Audrey brushed her hair back behind her ear. "Hey Hazel, when Zoe and I cleaned the attic, we found an old diary."

"You did? Who wrote it?" Finally, Hazel scooped some berries and cream into a clean bowl and tasted them, pulling back in surprise. "Mh-hmm. These *are* good."

"It's a bit of a mystery who wrote it." Zoe rose from her chair. She yawned and stretched luxuriously, then leisurely started to deadhead the yellow roses growing in a pot near the table. "So far, we only know it was somebody who loved rocks."

"Rocks? Like stones?"

"Yeah. Stones. And fossils."

"Did a kid write it?"

"Maybe. We haven't read many of the entries yet because the handwriting is that of a drunken ferret," Audrey added. "It hurts my eyes to look at it." Her phone pinged, and she checked the screen. A text from River. He had visited the local hospital and was on his way home, asking whether she wanted to take a walk over the bluff.

Audrey texted back that she had guests as well as berries and whipped cream, and to join them.

As soon as she had sent the text, a knock made her look up.

"Hello, darlings." Aunt Georgie stepped out of the living room and onto the patio. She was dressed in her beach-walking attire, wearing three-quarter pants, a white eyelet tunic, a wagon-wheel straw hat tied under her chin, and pink flip-flops. In her hand were her fabulous vintage sunglasses. "I had my window open and heard you talking down here." She pointed her glasses at Hazel. "You must be the wedding dress shopkeeper."

"I am." Hazel tilted her head. "Hello."

"You can call me Aunt Georgie. The rest of them do, so we might as well keep things easy."

"Um, all right." Hazel smiled. "Hello, Aunt Georgie. It's nice to meet you."

Aunt Georgie nodded and turned to Audrey. "What's this about a diary you found in the attic?"

"Oh, maybe you are able to tell us who wrote it," Audrey said eagerly. "We found a signature on the inside of the cover. It's hard to read, but we think it's either Marina or Marianne. Does that name ring any bells?"

"Marianne?" Aunt Georgie started to shake her head but suddenly stopped and blinked, her focus going inward. Then she frowned. "Does it really say Marianne?"

CHAPTER 13

Hazel put her spoon down, too interested in the conversation to eat. Listening, she glanced at the gable of the historic home. She loved flea markets and antique stores and old attics. They were places full of promise and mystery, and it would be a treat to climb a creaking staircase and rummage around Audrey's attic.

But of course, that was not possible. A recent acquaintance like her couldn't very well ask to snoop around another family's old things. There was something intimate and vulnerable about possessions that were stored away because their owners treasured and couldn't part with them.

Yet it sure would be fun to join Zoe and Audrey in finding diaries and deciphering them.

Hazel looked at Audrey, who'd gone to get the diary and was now returning to her chair, holding a faded green booklet in her hands.

Carefully, Audrey opened it, revealing the inside of the cover page.

"Look, Aunt Georgie. I'm fairly certain about the first part of the signature. The last part is all one loopy scrawl, but it could easily say Marianne. What do you think?"

Aunt Georgie pulled reading glasses from her pocket and set them on her nose. Then she leaned over the book. "Yes. That says Marianne." She picked it up and flipped through the pages, stopping here and there to decipher an entry. Finally, she shook her hand and returned the diary to Audrey. "Who taught that girl to write?" she muttered. "The letters look like a drunk sailor scratched the paper with a fingernail dipped in tar."

Zoe had finished deadheading the roses and came over to peek at the diary over Audrey's shoulder.

Hazel folded her hands, telling herself to stay seated even though she was burning for a glance. She'd volunteered both at the island's elementary school and the senior center. After unraveling the meaning behind so many loopy scrawls and slurred connectors, maybe she would be able to read the entries. But a journal was a private matter, so she held her breath and waited.

"Who is Marianne, Aunt Georgie?" Zoe asked, giving up on making sense of the scrawls. "Is it someone in the family?"

"I wish I knew," Aunt Georgie murmured and put her large sunglasses on.

"But you recognized the name." Audrey looked up.

"I don't know any Mariannes," Aunt Georgie assured her. "Not a single one."

"Maybe not personally." Audrey sighed. "But you know *something*, don't you?"

"Well…" Aunt Georgie took a breath that strained the eyelets of her tunic. "My mother did mention the name once. I wasn't supposed to hear it."

"Really?" Audrey's eyes widened. "Tell me more, please."

Aunt Georgie looked out at the beach, where the warm sand shimmered in the golden sun, stretching like a soft, tempting blanket down to the sea. "I heard her say the name here, on the beach. No, not say it… She was *calling* it. Out loud."

"She called it out loud?" Audrey tucked her chin.

"A couple of nights after my sister disappeared. Everyone was close to a nervous breakdown."

Audrey reached out, taking her aunt's hand into her own. "Why did your mother call the name?"

"I don't know." Aunt Georgie shrugged. "I never knew. But she was on the beach at night, calling into the rising wind. I saw her from my open window."

"What was she doing?"

"Nothing. She stood by a driftwood log and for the longest time just looked out at the ocean. I remember her hair was fluttering behind her."

"And then she called out for Marianne?"

"It could have been Mary Anne, I suppose." Aunt Georgie pushed her glasses back up and looked at Audrey. "She crossed her hands just below her throat, leaned into the wind, and called the name. Almost as if she was imploring Marianne for guidance, or… I don't know." She hesitated. "I felt like she was calling out for help. We were so desperate for someone to come and fix everything. All night, I was hoping Marianne would materialize and bring my sister back home. But she never did."

"Did you never ask your mom about it?"

Aunt Georgie shook her head. "I only cared about finding my sister. If my mother had wanted to tell me about Marianne, she would have. But I never heard her mention the name again."

"Oof." Zoe exhaled.

Aunt Georgie pointed at the journal. "Well, girls, now that you have found Marianne's diary... I'd like to hear who she was as soon as you figure it out."

"Of course." Audrey smiled. "You'll be the first to know."

"Who is the first to know what?" a deep voice asked from the side of the house.

Hazel felt an electric current zing through her chest as if the voice vibrated a string inside her heart. Her eyes met River's.

"Hey, River," Audrey said. "Join us."

"Hi, everyone." River took turns hugging his aunt, his sister, and Zoe.

Hazel held out her hand when River came over to greet her. But he ignored it and instead bent down to where she was sitting, pressing a light kiss on her cheek. "Welcome to the forgotten cove, stranger."

A startled "Oh!" escaped Hazel's lips. She pressed her fingertips to the spot.

"Was that too much? I apologize."

"I'm sorry, Hazel. Never mind my brother." Audrey shook her head at him. "He spent a year as an exchange student in Italy, and it's gone to his head. River, stop kissing people on the cheek, please. It's not as cute as you think it is."

Quickly, Hazel dropped her hand again. "No, it's fine," she said. "Of course it's fine."

"I'm sorry." River sounded more sincere now. "That was too much. I'm in a good mood. Clearly, too good."

Hazel smiled. "It's fine. I don't mind."

River pulled out the empty chair between her and Zoe and sat down. "So, is anyone going to answer my question?"

"What's your question again?" Zoe sat beside him and touched his arm. Clearly, she also felt the young doctor's charm.

"Who is this Marianne you were talking about?" River reached for an empty cup and filled it with coffee, taking a long drink before setting it back down.

Audrey pressed her palm flat on the diary on the table. "This is Marianne," she said. "We found her diary in the attic. But we can't read her handwriting."

"Um." Hazel cleared her throat. She couldn't keep quiet any longer. "I know it's none of my.... But I'm good with tricky hands. I've had lots of practice."

Audrey flashed Hazel a wide smile. "Why didn't you say so right away? Sounds like you're just the girl we need."

Zoe's phone pinged. "Shoot!" She jumped up. "Audrey, I have to go home right now. Dad's car died, and he needs mine to get to the San Jose airport ASAP."

Audrey rose too. "I thought you had an appointment in Pebble Beach. And you were going to go grocery shopping too."

"Yeah. I already pushed shopping back twice." Zoe huffed, exasperated. "We're running out of everything."

"Aunt Georgie and I will drive you," Audrey decided. "We meant to go to Pebble Beach anyway. Isn't that right, Aunt Georgie?"

"Sure. Why not." Aunt Georgie looked resignedly at the beach.

Audrey turned to Hazel. "I'm sorry about breaking up our coffee date. Unless you'd like to come along?"

Smiling, Hazel shook her head. She'd never meant to stay long for this first visit. "I should get back to the store."

Zoe was already pulling her purse strap over her shoulder, ready to leave. "You're not mad? I know Audrey was going to show you the house and everything."

Hazel stood, picking up her own purse. "Of course I'm not mad. It's no problem at all. Go get your dad to the airport. We'll meet again soon."

"Thank you." Spontaneously, Zoe hugged her.

Audrey picked up the diary and held it out for her. "Here. Take a shot at it, Hazel." Audrey, Aunt Georgie, and Zoe hurried inside, and a moment later, the sound of their cars could be heard rattling up Forgotten Lane.

Suddenly, Hazel was alone with River.

"I'd better get going as well," she said when that little fact sunk in. "I don't want to miss a customer."

"Can I ask you something, Hazel?" River rose.

"Like what?"

"There were only two cars in the driveway when I arrived. Now there's only one left, and that's mine."

"I was going to walk." It was an hour before her neighbor could pick her up.

"You are going to walk all the way back to Lover's Lane? In heels?" River rubbed his chin. "You'll get blisters. As a member of the medical profession, I can't endorse that. How about I give you a ride too?"

Hazel tugged her purse strap higher. The shoes did rub her heel... She'd put them on in case she'd meet him, so maybe it was only fair to accept the offer? She smiled, caught out. "I guess I would appreciate a ride. Thank you."

He raked his hand through his hair. "Good."

The warmth radiating from her chest spread to her throat as she smiled. This man *liked* helping people. And he liked *her*.

.

CHAPTER 14

When they had reached the cove's small marina port, River parked and then sat in his seat, humming under his breath to the music on the radio and looking out at the ferry positioning itself to dock.

Hazel reached for her door handle. "Thanks for the ride, River. I'm sorry I—"

He stopped humming and frowned at the clock on the car dash as if he hadn't heard her. "What sort of time is this for a boat to arrive? Did I download an outdated schedule on my phone?"

"The schedule is off. The business was sold recently, and they're improvising while they're working things out."

He nodded slowly. "My mother mentioned something like that."

"The lighthouse keeper's family used to own the ferry business. Now that he moved back here, he bought the ferry back. The old captain retired, and I think the new one hasn't arrived yet. Should be any day now."

"Good."

"A lot of islanders have their own boats, of course, but I'm not one of them." Hazel reached for the handle again.

"What are you doing?" River raised his eyebrows.

"I'm getting out." She tilted her head in question. "The ferry has arrived."

"But I'm driving you."

She blinked, confused. "You *have* driven me. Thank you very much. Now I have to take the ferry."

He pulled back, almost looking offended. "I'm driving you *all the way*, of course."

"All the way?" She dropped her hand. "River, you don't have to. Getting the car on the ferry is hardly worth it. I don't want to be an inconvenience. Honestly, I can easily take it from here."

It looked as if storm clouds gathered in his blue eyes. "It's no problem to get the car on the ferry since it drives itself. And you can't easily take it from here. Not in heels, Hazel. My sister would have my head if she learned I made you walk all the way from the harbor to Lover's Lane." A breath lifted his chest. "And Hazel—it's not an inconvenience. You are not an inconvenience. You couldn't be if you tried. Don't you know that?"

She stared at her hands. "I didn't mean... That's not what I meant." She felt herself blushing. Really, she had not meant to turn this into a thing about herself. He hadn't invited her to visit the old hotel, after all. She hadn't been River's guest. Obviously, it was her own responsibility to get herself back home.

The ferry had docked, and a crew member was waving them forward. There was space for two vehicles on the lower deck, but demand was low at this hour, and theirs was the only car waiting to get on.

"I know that's not what you meant." River started the engine, rolled onto the ferry, and parked in the assigned spot. It smelled of diesel fuel and warm metal corroded by sea salt and sun and speckled with barnacles. A small cormorant landed only a few feet ahead of them, flapping its wings for balance as it tried to grab the ferry's railing with its webbed feet.

River let down his window. "But I don't want you walking all that way. I *want* to drive you. It makes me feel good. Definitely better than putting my own feet up and wondering whether yours have blisters yet."

Hazel couldn't help but smile. "I walk all the time, River. Kitten heels or not. But thank you for caring."

He smiled back. "Life doesn't have to be hard. It's the little things that make the difference. So let's enjoy the ride. What do you think?"

"Let's enjoy the ride." Hazel also rolled down her window to let the fresh ocean air blow in. After being on her own for so long, even small favors could feel like taking on unnecessary debt.

Sitting beside River, Hazel decided she did not want to be someone who always counted favors, careful to keep her distance, so she didn't get in over her head.

Or her heart.

Soon, the ferry rumbled to life below them. He turned to her. "Would you like to get out and go to the upper deck?"

"Sure."

On the upper deck, they found an empty bench near the stern of the ferry. River sat down right beside her as if they were old friends, and for a while, they watched the mesmerizing quicksilver wake the ferry left as the hull pushed through the water. The sun was warm on Hazel's neck and shoulders. She inhaled deeply, feeling her heart widen.

Up here, the smell of fuel and metal was replaced by a clear, bright ocean breeze that promised beaches and waves and all the wonders of the underwater world.

"I love life in Mendocino already," River said after a while. "I understand why my mother came back."

"Where was she before she returned?"

"She lived in Portland, Maine. That's where I grew up. And before they moved there, my parents lived in Nantucket."

"I've seen pictures of Nantucket cottages overgrown with roses. I'd love to go and see them. I suppose you did?"

"Yes, I've visited often. The roses there really are something else." He smiled. "But there are flowers here too. Given how mild and sunny the winters here are, I'd say you have even more roses in Mendocino."

She liked how he effortlessly spun everything into joy. Instead of asking him for a favor, they suddenly enjoyed a spontaneous outing on the ocean. And instead of longing to travel, she suddenly felt like she had already arrived at the best place.

She smiled back at him. "We do have plenty of flowers. And I love living here too."

"Where *do* you live, Hazel?" he asked. "On top of the store?"

"Yes. There's a little apartment. It's small but cute."

He nodded. "Is it loud in the evenings? I imagine you have a lot of tourists in Lover's Lane."

"Sometimes. But it's a good thing. Tourists keep us in business. Though in the last two years, fewer people have visited the island. The drought kept them away."

He stood and leaned onto the railing, letting the sea breeze tousle his brown hair. "That can't be easy for a store."

"It's not." Hazel shrugged. She didn't want to talk about how much every sale counted. Especially since she had denied one to his mother.

"River?" a female voice called from the ferry's staircase. "Hazel!"

Hazel turned around. Smiling brightly, Billie Donovan was coming toward them. She was wearing a sweater to ward off the ocean's slipstream, and her short, curly hair blew in all directions.

"Hello, Billie." River greeted his mother's friend. "You are on your way to the island too?"

"Yep." Billie had reached them and was looking from River to Hazel and back. "I'm going to the lighthouse with Neil. He's the island's lighthouse keeper." She pointed over her shoulder at the wheelhouse. "He's also helming the ferry since his son hasn't arrived yet."

"Is his son the new captain?" River asked. "I didn't know."

Billie flashed him a smile. "There's a lot you don't know yet, kiddo. Anyways. How was your day?"

"Great." River crossed his arms. "I went to the hospital to introduce myself. It never hurts to know there's an extra set of hands if they're needed."

"Good." Billie raised an eyebrow. "And? Did they offer you a job? They always seem to be short-staffed."

River chuckled and shook his head. "The wheels of hospital administration don't turn that fast. They are interested, but the earliest they could hire me is at least a year from now."

Billie seemed crestfallen. "Can you stay that long?"

"It's not ideal, and they can't guarantee that it will happen. I'm afraid playing the waiting game that long is too big of a gamble."

"Oh no." The words escaped Hazel before she could stop herself. "Do you have to leave Mendocino Cove again? I thought you said you had good news."

It took him a moment before he answered. "The good news is that there is a chance I can come back. There *is* a hospital in town, after all, they are interested, and I did like everyone I met. It's still a win, isn't it?"

"So you would like to stay if you could?" Billie asked, interested.

"Sure." He looked out across the blue ocean. "It's beautiful here, and this is where my family is. My sister and great-aunt run the hotel in Mendocino Cove, and my mother teaches at the local university. It would make sense for me to settle here as well. I don't enjoy being lonely."

"Ah." Billie nodded wisely. "Of course you don't. Jenny told me about your engagement."

"I didn't know you were engaged," Hazel said quietly. It seemed a relevant piece of information. Accepting a ride from a charming young doctor was one thing. Accepting a ride from a charming young doctor who was engaged to be married was another thing. Especially when they freely kissed one's cheek and made one warm around the heart by being kind and helpful and handsome.

"Well, he's not." Billie beamed at her, clearly delighted. "She said no. Right, River?"

He turned away. "Yes. That's right."

"I'm so sorry," Hazel said sincerely. She remembered all her own painful breakups, and none of her relationships had been that serious.

"Ah well." His shoulders rose and fell as he sighed. "Better now than later."

"Sure." Billie cleared her throat as if she only now recognized how sensitive the topic was. "I'm sorry, River. You'll find someone else." She scratched her arm. "Actually, I came over to talk to you about a friend."

"A friend?" River turned back. His face had changed. The joy was gone from his eyes. "What friend is this?"

"His name is Terry. Henderson. He's a general practitioner in the cove." Billie shivered, rubbing her arms for warmth. "I should say *the* general practitioner since he's the only one. He's had a few health issues lately. Nothing too bad, but he could use help."

"He could?"

"I was thinking it would be a good idea to introduce you to him too. What do you think?"

River nodded. "I'd like to meet him. I might be able to give him a hand while I'm in town."

"He's at the lighthouse right now to pick up some books. How long are you planning to be on the island?"

River rubbed his jaw. "I was going to drop off Hazel and head back to help Jon with the new house."

"Jon won't mind if you take a few minutes to say hi to Terry. What do you think? You could meet me there."

"How do I get to the lighthouse?"

"I know the way," Hazel said. "I can show you."

There were no potential customers on the empty ferry. No young couple holding hands or gaggles of girl-friends had boarded the ferry, no mother and daughter teams talking about sweetheart necklines and ruffles. It wouldn't matter if the store stayed closed while Hazel took her turn helping River.

"All right. Thanks." He smiled at her.

She smiled. *All right. Thanks.* That's how easy it was.

CHAPTER 15

Hazel leaned her head back into her neck and squinted up at the crystal-blue sky. The old lighthouse rose majestically, the windows of the beacon room proudly reflecting the October sun.

Not so long ago, the lighthouse keeper had given a fundraising ball here. He'd had a band and dancing and everything. Hazel's few remaining friends all went with their families or partners, and Hazel knew better than to be a third wheel. But now, she wished she'd have come anyway.

Billie knocked on the heavy wooden door, then pushed it open. Hazel could tell that she was comfortable here.

"Terry?" Billie called up the winding staircase. Then she entered. "He can't hear well. Come on in, kids. He must be upstairs."

River let Hazel go ahead and closed the door behind them.

"It's pretty in here. I had no idea it was so cozy." Hazel looked around the cozy entrance hall. The old wood floor, polished by many feet to a warm sheen, gleamed in the rays of sunlight falling through the windows. Antique, sturdy furniture, framed pictures of sailboats out on sea, and a large vase full of fall flowers completed the look.

"I like it." River stood close behind her.

Hazel could feel the warmth of his body on the skin of her arms. Involuntarily, she inhaled the air as if it were water and she was thirsty. River smelled of sandalwood and something clean, like fresh linen on a bed.

They followed Billie up the winding staircase and into a living room with a small fireplace. On the sofa in front of it sat a tall, thin man, his shoulders hunched over the book that lay open on his knees.

"Terry?" Billie went to him, putting a hand on his shoulder.

Dr. Henderson looked up, and when he saw Billie, his frown of concentration changed into a smile of recognition. "Billie, dear. There you are," he said in a low, gravelly voice that sounded like moving rocks in a riverbed. "I've waited for you."

Billie waved River to come forward.

Hazel, too, stepped into the room, smiling. She knew the old man well. He'd been her doctor all her life. His hearing had been getting worse for years, and it had finally gotten to a point where he was more lip-reading than hearing his patients.

"Terry, this young man here is the son of a friend," Billie said and slipped her arm through River's.

"Nice to meet you, Dr. Henderson. I'm River Summers."

"Hello, young man." Dr. Henderson pulled the heavy book off his lap and onto the sofa. Gripping the armrest, he rose to his full height and extended his hand. "Good to meet you. Is this your first time on our little island? How do you like it?"

River smiled. "I like your island very much. I've already fallen head over heels for the coastline, and there has been at least one sunset I'll never forget."

"Yes." Dr. Henderson laughed and shook River's hand again. "That's how it goes."

Billie smiled. "River is a newly minted doctor. A general practitioner, as luck has it."

"Really?" Terry's chin tilted back, and he gave River a sharp, appraising look that was nothing like his mild gaze before.

River straightened his shoulders. "Yes, newly minted and certified."

"I see." The sharp gaze mellowed just as suddenly as it had come, and Dr. Henderson nodded thoughtfully. "Well now. Are you any good?"

River told him a few hospitals and numbers and names, none of which meant anything to Hazel.

But Dr. Henderson's eyebrows rose, and he pursed his lips in approval. "Good. I suppose little Billie here has told you that I've run into a spot of trouble with my hearing?"

"Little Billie is going to turn fifty soon," Billie said briskly. "And she hasn't said much of anything to the kid. I thought I'd leave that to you, Terry." She let go of River. "Here, why don't we sit down?"

"Ah. Yes." Dr. Henderson looked down at the sofa as if he was appraising the distance.

"Let me..." River took his hand and helped the old doctor down.

"Thank you. I think I like you, young man." Dr. Henderson let out a low breath of relief as he leaned back into the pillows. Clearly, his hearing wasn't the only thing that needed relief.

River looked around. "Hazel? Would you like to sit?"

"I..." She couldn't very well stand by the door if everyone else was seated, chatting comfortably. "All right," she said. "Thanks."

She took the seat beside Dr. Henderson. Billie and River each sat in one of the cozy armchairs. Then the two doctors, the old and the young, started talking shop, beginning with Dr. Henderson's struggles with rheumatoid arthritis and hearing loss, brushing River's impressions of the cove's hospital, and ending with a long exchange about baffling patient cases.

Hazel zoned in and out of paying attention to the conversation. It was interesting, but there also were other things to think about.

For example, the room itself, so warm and comfortable and with a to-die-for view of the glittering ocean. Or the way Billie moved around confidently in the space, bringing pots of tea and plates of shortcake and cookies, rearranging the dahlias in their pretty green glass vase and joining the discussion now and then before pottering off again. It was clear she was the lady of the house.

"Are you okay?" Billie asked her once in a quiet aside, and Hazel nodded and said yes, she very much was, and she was enjoying herself. Another time, Billie wanted Hazel's opinion on the marzipan cookies, and a little later, she wondered about Hazel's four most favorite books. The men talked on, undisturbed and deeply engrossed in their conversation.

Finally, Billie checked her phone. "It's *late*!" she exclaimed and laughed when everyone looked up. "I'm sorry, I didn't mean to startle you. It's just a lot later than I thought it was. Terry, I promised to return you to your wife in time. We really need to get going."

Groaning over his stiff knees, Dr. Henderson rose. River and Hazel stood as well, supporting him left and right. "Well, it was a pleasure to see you again, little Hazel," Dr. Henderson said when he was standing. "I apologize if we've bored you. It's not often I get to drone on about work."

"I'm glad you got the chance," Hazel said. She meant it; the old doctor was one of her favorite people on the island. "Let me know if you need anything. I'm always around."

"Sure." He patted her hand, and then he turned to River. "Help me down the steps, River. I swear they get steeper every time."

"You've got it." River readily supported the old doctor.

Billie looped her arm through Hazel's, and together, they followed the two men. Then Billie locked the lighthouse's front door and waved goodbye to River and Hazel standing at the door.

"Whew." River ran a hand through his hair as Billie's truck drove away.

Hazel glanced at River. "Did you enjoy meeting the good doctor?" She smiled.

"He's great."

"Is that a yes?"

He looked at her, surprised. "Total yes. I wish I had met him earlier." His lips tugged into a grin. "I'm also sorry if we've bored you, by the way. I didn't mean to do that."

"You didn't bore me." Hazel smiled. "If Billie hadn't happened to check the time, we'd all still be sitting up there, happy as clams."

"You were happy as a clam, listening to us going on?"

She nodded, and then she took a few steps into the garden that surrounded the old lighthouse. "How pretty is this?" she murmured and turned a blossom of a blooming heritage rose so she could admire the soft yellow petals.

At one time, this garden had been well cared for.

But now, untended, overgrown, and dipped into the warm glow of the sinking sun, it was full of a wild beauty that was more magical than tended beds and clear lines.

River had come to stand behind her. "Here are the roses you wanted."

She smiled over her shoulder. "Should we go now? I don't want to keep you any longer."

"More like, I kept you. If it weren't for you, I wouldn't have met Dr. Henderson."

Hazel laughed. "You live in the cove, don't you? It's only a matter of time until you meet everyone." She turned back to the roses, but he suddenly leaned over her, enveloping her in his scent.

Hazel held her breath. What was he doing?

"Sorry," he whispered, his mouth right beside her ear, and then he reached past her and picked the rose she had admired.

"Hey!" Startled, she turned to tell him he couldn't pick the lighthouse keeper's roses. But she'd not realized just how close he was. She had to tilt her head and let her eyes travel from his chest to his eyes.

His lips curled into a smile when she finally met his gaze. "Yes?"

"You can't pick the lighthouse roses," she whispered. It didn't feel important all of a sudden.

"But this one is yours." He held the rose into the narrow gap left between them. "Here."

Without being able to think, she took it. Their fingers met, and he didn't let go.

"Are you afraid?" he asked softly.

"What if he gets angry?" Not because she thought the lighthouse keeper would notice a single missing rose when he had so many blooming in his garden. But she had to say something. Anything. Any words to break the spell that held her.

"Then I'll fight him for your rose," River murmured and leaned down. Gently, he kissed Hazel's forehead.

She blinked, finally waking up. Before she could say anything, River had already let go, stepped back, and turned toward the ocean, leaving her standing with a rose and a burning spot on the forehead.

"I should properly thank you, Hazel," he said over his shoulder, letting the breeze carry the words to her. "Dr. Henderson suggested that I take over his praxis while he's undergoing a procedure to help his hearing."

It took Hazel a moment before she could speak. "He really said that?" She had missed it while talking to Billie about marzipan and books.

He nodded, still not looking at her. "Yes. I didn't expect anything like it."

"I'm glad." Hazel swallowed. River would stay in Mendocino, then? How long would it take Dr. Henderson to take care of himself? A week or two? Did the old doctor want to take a short vacation, or a long one, or—

Abruptly, River turned. "Ready to go?"

"Uh." She tilted her head at the sudden change in his eyes and voice. "Sure."

"All right." Walking past her, River strode toward the car.

Hazel followed him, getting into the passenger seat. She cast a last look at the sun sinking into the ocean before she closed her door. The sky was streaked with gold and fire, and the air over here, away from the roses, smelled of salt and blooming heather. Two gulls were flying across the burning sky, calling to each other.

"So, how do we get from here to your place?" River started the car, ignoring the untamed beauty around them.

"Right." She cleared her throat. The skin where he'd kissed her felt like it shimmered in the falling dark. Hazel rubbed it with a finger to make the feeling go away. "Down here and left." She pointed.

"Right," he murmured, and then he drove, not talking again until they reached Lover's Lane.

CHAPTER 16

River parked by the small bridge that led across the babbling creek.

"Thank you for the ride." Hazel unbuckled and opened her door. It had been a short, strange drive. She didn't expect to be entertained. But she also hadn't expected to be kissed on the forehead. It seemed like once that happened, you had to follow up with a sentence or two.

"Hazel."

One foot already on the pavement, she turned. River was studying his hands. "Yes?" There was a coolness in the single word she hadn't meant to let shine through.

River looked up. It took him so long to speak that Hazel's eyebrows rose. "Do you know when the next ferry leaves?"

"Oh." She lowered her eyebrows. It used to be every hour on the hour, but now, nobody really knew when the next ferry left. "Hang on." She pulled out her phone and looked up the website. "It does say two hours." She let her phone sink to look at him.

He frowned. "Two hours?"

"I know. It's a long time to wait." Of course, River could eat something in one of the small restaurants or cafés lining the sea. But despite his new silence, it seemed rude, sending him to wait on his own. He was on the island because of her kitten heels, after all.

She turned the stem of her rose between her fingers. "Would you like to come in, River? We can have a glass of wine. And I have leftover lasagna if you're hungry."

To her relief, his cool facade finally cracked, and the corner of his lips lifted. "Leftover lasagna?"

She shrugged lightly. "It's the best kind. Don't you know that?"

The corners lifted higher. "I'd love some. I'm starving. The marzipan cookies sent my blood sugar sky high, and now..." He looked up, meeting her gaze. "Now, I'm crashing," he said quietly. "I'm falling. And I don't want to. Not right now."

"Oh. Maybe you need some protein." Hazel had eaten the same cookies, and her blood sugar seemed just fine. Billie had even said she'd halved the amount of sugar in the recipe. But everyone's body was different, and maybe River hadn't eaten a good breakfast.

She got out of the car. "All right, come on. We only have to walk over the bridge. It's not far. Not even for someone with low blood sugar."

She heard River get out and close the door, and together, they walked onto the bridge. The love locks on the railing, left by the many couples visiting Lover's Lane, shimmered gold and silver in the afterglow of the sun.

When they reached the top of the bridge, River stopped and leaned on the railing, watching the creek below. The water was a velvety blackish blue in the falling dark, speckled with light where there were lit windows in the nearby houses.

Hazel joined him. She put her hands on the cold metal. With the sun, the warmth of the day had left the air, and she shivered in her thin dress. "I can hear the creek in my room," she said, preoccupied with how cold she was. "It's like a lullaby for falling asleep."

He shrugged off his jacket and hung it over her shoulders. "October's here. Let's go inside before you freeze."

Grateful, Hazel pulled the jacket tighter. "Thank you. I forgot how cool October nights can get."

"Mh-mm." He put an arm around her and led her over the bridge.

Hazel went without protesting. Maybe he really was just a doctor at heart, eager to get her inside so she wouldn't catch a runny nose. The kiss—and the rose—could have simply been a sign of his good mood after the cozy meeting in the lighthouse.

"Uh, here it is." Hazel stopped at her door.

He dropped his arm and looked up at the gable. "I could have sworn it was further down the lane."

"I promise this is it." She smiled at him. "Lasagna, here we come. Don't get shaky now. It won't take long to heat up." She unlocked the door and flipped on the switch. One by one, like a warm wave rolling through the store, soft lights flickered to life.

River closed the door behind them, and Hazel locked it again.

"That's where Faye fell," he murmured absent-mindedly as they passed the changing rooms.

"Oof." Hazel closed her eyes and dropped her keys on the counter. "Please don't remind me. I was so scared for her baby."

He laughed quietly, and she opened her eyes again, smiling back. "You did good," he said. "And she is all right."

"Is she?" Hazel wanted to hear it again. Maybe that way, some day in the future, she also could laugh about the fall. "I thought she twisted her ankle."

"Not even. It only needs some rest and some ice. I checked on her this morning, and she's walking around without crutches. She was only worried about the baby."

"And the baby is fine?"

"The baby is fine."

Hazel exhaled. "I'm so glad. I'd have never forgiven myself if something had happened." When she looked up, River was smiling.

"You care, don't you?" he asked.

"Of course I care. Who wouldn't?"

"Lots of people don't care."

"I'm sure somewhere deep inside, they do. Maybe they aren't able to show it." She went to the staircase that led to the apartment. "Careful that you don't twist an ankle too." She switched the store lights off. The only light illuminating the sales floor now came from the rising moon that shone through the shop windows. "I meant to replace the light bulb but never got around to it." She started climbing the dark stairs.

River followed her. "You don't want Faye to fall, but you're okay falling yourself?"

"But I'm *not* falling," she pointed out. "I grew up in this house and know every step and stair. I can easily find my way around in total darkness without a problem."

"You should have a light," he insisted. "This is a safety hazard."

Hazel pushed open the door to her home and went inside. "I promise to fix it, doctor. Soon as I get around to buying a bulb."

"I'll buy lightbulbs if you promise to use them." River followed Hazel into the small apartment and closed the door to the staircase.

CHAPTER 17

"Welcome to my place." Hazel shrugged out of River's jacket, handing it back to him. With an apologetic glance, she slipped out of her heels. "Sorry. Not a minute longer."

He slung his jacket over his arm, watching her with a smile on his lips. "I figured."

Hazel was used to being alone up here. He filled the room, making it appear smaller than usual. She went into the kitchen and opened the fridge, sensing the moment he entered behind her without having to look. "It'll be quick. Have a seat." She pulled out the foil-covered dish and turned on the stove.

"Can I move these?"

She turned to see that he was pointing at the pile of fashion magazines and design books on the bench under the window. "Yes. Please. Here." She hurried over, taking the piles from his hands and putting them, after brief consideration, on the only chair.

"Where are you going to sit?" he asked, interested.

"I'm going to heat up the lasagna."

"But when you're done?"

Hazel had to laugh. "Then I'll find another spot. Do you want a glass of wine?"

"Goodness, yes. Thank you for asking." His aloofness from the car seemed to have left now that he was in her space.

Relieved, Hazel pulled her only bottle out from under the sink and dusted it off with her sleeve, then inspected it critically. "It's red."

"You keep your wine under the sink?" He smiled.

"Um. Yes?" She chuckled, a little embarrassed. "I don't have a wine cellar, sir."

"Red sounds like just the thing I need."

"Fair warning. I don't know if it's any good. I don't know the first thing about wines."

"Can I see?" He held out his hand, and she gave him the bottle, then went to find glasses.

"I only have water tumblers. I'm not much of a drinker."

"This is a great year," he said, with respect in his voice. "Where did you buy this?"

"It was a gift," she admitted. "A good friend gave it to me."

"What good friend?" He reached for the corkscrew she was holding out. "Your boyfriend?" He lowered his chin and paused what he was doing to look at her.

"My boyfriend?" She tilted her head. "No."

"Hmm." River opened the bottle. "I mean...it's none of my business, of course."

Hazel pulled on a mitt and opened the oven, then pushed the glass dish inside. Luckily, there was enough left for a decent dinner. "A salad would be nice." She closed the stove and went back to the fridge. "Nope," she muttered, glancing inside. "Maybe next time."

River was flipping through one of her design books.

"Um, I don't have any lettuce."

"Did you make all these notes in the margins?" He pointed at a page abundantly sprinkled with black scribbles in Hazel's hand.

She smiled. "I must've. They don't sell them like that."

He smiled back. "So you are...what, exactly? A tailor?"

"A dressmaker," she told him. "I make dresses."

"Like the one you are wearing?" He raised an appraising eyebrow, but his eyes stayed on hers instead of slipping down her dress.

"Yes, like this one. But I only sell wedding gowns."

"You make wedding gowns too?"

"When I'm able to buy the materials, anyway," she admitted. "This year has not been good for sales. But I have an atelier downstairs, and wedding gowns are my favorites. I also sell other vintage gowns because I adore it when a woman wants to share her special dress with someone else. It's love that really makes a dress special."

"Love?"

"Yes." She nodded. "I only take on lucky dresses. Their owners remember the love they felt when they wore them and want another woman to have the same good luck in marriage." Hazel sighed happily. "Some very special dresses have changed hands in this store. Each one comes with its own story."

"I see. Only lucky, happy dresses, then."

She grinned. "Don't you dare laugh at me."

"I'm not." He laughed softly. "I'm not."

"Sure. Why don't you pour the wine?"

"Yes, ma'am." Still smiling, he poured the wine into Hazel's water glasses and handed her one. "We don't need salad. Sit with me." River unceremoniously lifted the stack of magazines off the second chair and sat it on the ground beside the bench.

"Thanks. I need to get a third chair, obviously." Hazel sat and clicked her glass to his.

"Can I just..." River set down his glass.

"Hmm?" She puckered her lips, the wine tart in her mouth.

Unaffected himself, River smiled. "Can I just make sure—you aren't seeing anyone, are you?"

She set her glass down. Maybe it was payback for the silence earlier that made her want to draw him out. "Why?"

He shrugged. "I'd hate for someone to come storming up the stairs, mad because I'm having a glass of wine with his woman."

"And lasagna," she reminded him.

"And lasagna."

"No." She stood, taking her glass with her to the stove. "Nobody is going to come storming up the stairs. Can I also ask you something?"

"Yes." River straightened his back.

"You didn't talk to me on the drive over here." She pulled on her oven mitts and took the glass dish out, poking it with a fork. The cheese was bubbly and melted, and the delicious scent of basil and self-made marinara filled the air. "Why not?"

"Because..." River ran a hand through his hair. "I didn't know what to do."

"To do? Did you have to do anything?"

"I'm used to it," he said briefly before falling silent once again.

Hazel brought plates and silverware to the table, then cut the lasagna and served them both a piece. "River?" She sat down and propped her chin in her hand.

"Hmm?" He looked up. A small frown was playing on his face.

"You are doing it again."

"What?"

"Not talking." Hazel took her fork and then set it down again. "I wouldn't mind, only...you kissed me on the forehead and gave me a rose." She pressed her lips together. "And the next minute, you don't talk to me. Then you ask me if I have a partner. And then you fall silent again." She took a breath. "I'm getting mixed signals. And I can't handle mixed signals because I'm not an on-off sort of person."

"Sorry. I'm sorry, Hazel. I don't mean to do that." He rubbed his hands over his face.

"No, that's not..." Hazel wasn't looking for an apology. She wanted to talk. "I'm just trying to understand what is happening," she said softly.

River dropped his hands. "Me too. I'm trying really hard to understand."

She reached out, putting her hand on his. "Maybe it's because I live in a world of weddings and true love. But I'm not good at playing around with my heart, River. Or yours, for that matter." She paused for a moment. When he didn't say anything, she pulled her hand back again. "Let's just be friends, okay? No more roses and kisses."

River pulled his hand back as well. "Yeah. Yeah, I think that's a good idea." He looked up. "I'm sorry about the mixed messages, Hazel. I shouldn't have done that."

She picked up her fork, ready to change the topic. They'd talked enough about love and wedding dresses. "You were great, jumping into action and saving Faye that day. Really. Like a superhero without a cape. I was impressed."

"I didn't do anything more than bring her to the hospital."

"You made everyone feel safe."

"You did too."

"I was running around with my hands waving frantically in the air. At least that's what it felt like." Hazel sighed at the memory.

"That's what all accidents feel like."

They started to talk about River's work, getting back to eating and sipping the wine.

Eventually, River looked at his phone. "If I want to catch the ferry, I should leave," he said. "Thank you for the company and the delicious dinner, Hazel."

She stretched and yawned. She'd had barely half her glass, but she noticed a warm, heavy feeling settling over her. "Thank you for the ride, River. It was a fun day."

He stood. "It was quite the detour, wasn't it? Next time, I promise to bring you straight home."

She dropped her arms. "Listen, do you mind taking me to the harbor? I didn't go shopping, and our little market store is already closed. I want to buy a pastry for breakfast tomorrow in one of the harbor cafés."

"How can I deny a woman a pastry?" The corners of his eyes crinkled.

She leaned her elbows on the table and smiled back. "The two of us are going to be very good friends, River."

CHAPTER 18
The Past

Her heart hammering in her chest, Marianne slipped down the cliff. She knew where to set her feet and which roots held and which ones gave. But if Klara had spotted her, she would think Marianne had fallen off the edge.

Marianne ducked under a rock shelf, waiting with bated breath. If she'd been seen, Klara would surely yell out for her.

Marianne closed her eyes, again seeing the words she had scrawled into her diary the night before.

The wedding is coming closer. Today, I had to try on the dress my future mother-in-law made for me. It was beautiful, and she was excited, but all I could think of was the way Robert would look at me. It made my skin crawl. A couple of days ago, he told me I was too pretty and that I should not go out on my own anymore now that I was engaged. Tears rose to my eyes when I pictured myself walking down the aisle toward him. Klara saw it. She said to Mama, look how happy she is. A real bride, she's blushing.

But I wasn't blushing. I was hot with terror. I left as soon as I could and went home to take a long bath in the middle of the day.

Marianne bit her lip so hard she tasted blood. Then she counted to twenty, whispering the numbers into the wind.

There was no cry of discovery. Her knees started to ache from her awkward, cramped position. She moved, revealing her hiding spot. Still, Klara's voice did not rise over the rushing of waves and the cawing of the gulls.

What were the chances of Klara walking this way just now? It wasn't the most direct way to the ferry, or the market, or anything at all. The narrow path up the cliff was good only for picking huckleberries. And October was no longer a time for berries.

Marianne adjusted her position again and lifted her skirt to inspect her leg. In her hasty scramble down the cliff, the blade of the small shovel she'd held hidden in the folds of her dress had scratched up her ankle. Tessie would not tattle about a bloodied stocking. She was used to them.

Marianne pulled Mama's pin from her hair and pinned up the skirt, no longer in need of folds to hide equipment. Carefully, she climbed down the last of the cliff and soon reached the rocky beach below. Where the rugged coast met the ocean here, the waves crashed and reared like wild horses. Marianne knew never to turn her back to the sea. Sneaky waves had sucked more than one woman into the sea, taking her hostage forever over a quick basket of mussels for dinner.

Keeping a watchful eye on her unpredictable blue friend, Marianne gripped her shovel tighter. According to the map, the cave opening was at the end of a slippery path over roughly hewn boulders that lay toppled together as if thrown down by a giant's hand. Between the boulders lay large tidepools that were covered with thick mats of black seaweed.

Marianne liked her bones, and she liked them intact. She had no intention of breaking as much as a toe, and she never before had dared such a dangerous climb. But pirates didn't bury treasure where children built their sandcastles. It took at least wet skirts to get the prize.

Shovel in hand, she started to make her way over the rocky beach until she reached the boulders. After a short study of the possible paths ahead, she pulled off her boots and stockings. She tied the laces together and knotted everything into her belt. A gull screamed somewhere above as if it tried to give her away, but when Marianne squinted into the azure sky, the cliff was empty. No scandalized Klara. Only the wind that rustled the feathery arms of a beach cypress.

Marianne stepped onto the bed of algae. The blistery layers slithered treacherously beneath her feet. Using the shovel as a crutch, she worked her way forward, pausing every so often to assess the rolling, crashing sea or wipe the spray from her face. More than once she told herself that if she didn't turn back this moment, the next she would fall victim to her overactive imagination. Just as Robert had predicted when she had tried to tell him about her fossil hunting.

Marianne narrowed her eyes. She had not liked his tone when he said it.

Using her shovel, she probed the depth of the seaweed ahead and took another step. The blade slipped, and with a cry, Marianne fell. Unable to stop herself, she slid toward the greedy sea until she slammed into a barnacle-blistered rock. A large wave drenched her in icy water, and Marianne gasped, clawing at the sharp rock for a hold, anything, so she wouldn't wash into the ocean. But the water tugged relentlessly, wrapping her long skirt around its shapeless hands and dragging her like a felled log. A smaller wave came to help, but Marianne managed at the last moment to dig her bleeding fingers into a thick braid of algae. Gasping for air, she watched the wave recede again.

This time, the sea had only claimed her shovel.

Half sitting, half walking, she hastily climbed toward the beach, back to where she'd first fallen. For a while she rested there, shivering with shock. Then, wincing, she rose to her feet and inspected herself. Her fingers and knuckles were white as chalk, but soon, the scrapes would turn painful. Her bare feet were also in poor shape. The wet skirt mercilessly rubbed salt into the scratches that the barnacles had left.

Marianne didn't enjoy pain. She liked adventures and discoveries, not injuries and broken bones.

Pursing her lips and exhaling the pain as best she could, Marianne slowly climbed her way back to the rocky beach. She needed to make a fire to dry herself before walking back home. Even taking shortcuts only she knew, there were places and crossings where someone might spot her in her dirty, sandy, crumpled frock that smelled of brine and smoke. But still better to say she had fallen asleep next to a bonfire than to admit the ocean had almost sucked her into an early grave.

Her fingers searing with the pain of abrasions, Marianne grabbed a head of seaweed and pulled herself onto the beach. She braced her hands on her knees and bent over to catch her breath.

When she straightened, she was smiling. She'd made it back. It was fine. Nothing broken, nothing lost. Skin healed quickly. And Grandmama had definitely been through worse. Tessie would be angry, but she would also help Marianne clean up and bring her a bowl of chicken soup.

Marianne shook her hair back, wiping wet strands out of her eyes.

Then she blinked.

Had she just seen a person up on the cliff?

Shading her eyes against the sun, she squinted at the beach cypresses. A black shadow had ducked behind the tree closest to the spot where she'd jumped down to avoid Klara. Marianne was sure of it.

For a long time, she stood staring at the tree trunks.

But nothing moved, and nobody called out to ask what she was doing.

Finally, she lowered her hand. She had better start that fire instead of watching for people flapping around behind trees like ghosts.

Marianne gathered dry driftwood and sticks, then took flint and steel from her pocket. Spurring sparks, she cast a quick glance toward the slippery path leading to the cave.

It *was* a good hiding spot.

Next time, she would wear sturdy boots. And bring a thick, long stick. That would get her across the seaweed.

Marianne added a sun-bleached twig to the licking flames, pursed her lips, and started to whistle a cheerful shanty.

Chapter 19

I'm sorry, River." The cool breeze coming in from the ocean blew Hazel's hair in her face. She shook it back.

River was still staring at the yellow note stuck to the glass case by the ferry dock.

When he turned to her, there was a deep line between his eyes. "Change of ownership or not, I wish they'd stop changing the schedule without notice."

"I know." Hazel leaned forward and read the note again. The last boat of the day had left half an hour ago.

River was stuck on the island. "Erm." He looked over his shoulder at the row of lit harbor cafés and restaurants, then back at her. "What now? What do people do if they need to get to the cove?"

"They take their own boats," Hazel replied and pulled her coat closer around herself. October days could be lovely and warm, but the nights were another thing.

Distracted, he reached out and tucked a floating strand of hair behind her ear. "What do they do if they don't have a boat?"

"I suppose they stay on the island."

River raised an eyebrow. "What if it's an emergency?"

"The hospital also owns a boat."

"So I'll have to call the hospital to get back home?"

"If it's an emergency." She tilted her head and smiled.

"But it's not...exactly that." He looked at her. "It's not exactly a medical emergency."

"And the hospital won't thank the new doctor in town for ordering the boat because he missed the last ferry." She wanted to take his hand but didn't. "Hey. It's not the end of the world. People get stuck on the wrong side all the time."

"So what do they do? There's no hotel."

She smiled. "They stay the night with friends, I suppose. They catch a ferry the next morning."

"Ah." He shoved his hands in his pockets. "You're cold. Let's go grab a hot drink to warm up." He nodded toward the bright line of lit windows.

They went to the café where Hazel had been before. She shrugged off her coat and hung it up while River ordered hot chocolate and iced carrot cake from the bored Brooklyn barista.

"Here." River set a steaming mug in front of Hazel and made another trip to get the cake. "I didn't mean to make you stand around in the cold and solve my problems."

"I don't mind." She tried the carrot cake. It was soft and juicy, with candied walnuts and a fresh cream cheese frosting with just the right amount of sweetness. "This is delicious."

"Good." He smiled. "Maybe I'll get a piece to keep me company in the car tonight."

"River, just stay with me." Hazel put her fork down. "Don't spend the night in your car. That's silly. And uncomfortable."

"Stay with you?" His eyebrows rose so high that Hazel had to laugh.

"Yes. We settled that we are friends, didn't we? I promise I won't try anything." She winked.

He hesitated. "Are you sure? I've slept in worse places than a car."

"Like what?"

"Like a hospital broom closet. Very crowded."

She shook her head. "Of course I'm sure. We'll watch a movie and have another glass of wine. You can tell me about all those bad places you slept in."

He sucked in a breath. "First, we should settle exactly where I'll sleep tonight."

The intensity of his gaze made Hazel lower her own eyes. "A camping mattress. You can put it wherever you like. Even the store, if you prefer wedding dresses over my snores."

"Hmm." River tried his cake. "Do you really snore?"

She shrugged. "According to my ex, anyway."

"Hey—I don't mind if you do. I think it's kind of cute."

"Really?"

He nodded. "But snoring can be a sign of a medical condition. Maybe I'll sleep upstairs to listen a little. Make sure you're okay."

Hazel smiled. "You want to diagnose my snoring?"

"Yes."

She shook her head, amused. "I'm not sure I can afford your fees."

"I have a sliding scale. My service for a camping mattress."

Hazel lifted her warm mug and sipped the creamy drink, trying not to think too much about the services River might offer.

"I'd take him up on it," the barista called out. "Free healthcare? It's a yes from me!"

Hazel shook her head, but she liked the way River chuckled to himself.

"Well." He leaned across the table so the nosy barista wouldn't hear. "Between the two of us, there's a hidden fee."

"What's that?" She smiled.

"Another glass of wine. That's on top of the mattress, of course."

Hazel leaned forward as well. "That's not a hidden cost," she whispered back. "I already offered."

For a moment, River's eyes dropped to her lips. "There's always a hidden cost," he murmured. He was so close. He had to feel the heat shooting into her sensitive skin.

"You guys almost finished?" The barista yawned loudly. "I don't mind calling it a day, if you know what I mean."

Abandoning his cake, River stood. "Ma'am?"

"What?"

"Do you still have pastries to sell?"

"Tons. Enough for all of Brooklyn."

"Brooklyn? Why Brooklyn?" River went to the counter, pulling out his wallet. Moments later, he returned. "Here." River handed Hazel a white paper bag, then helped her into her coat. "Wrap up warm, or you'll catch a cold after all."

"Yes, Doctor." Hazel couldn't help but smile. It'd been years since someone cared about her catching a cold. "What's in here?"

"Our breakfast." He held out his hand for hers. "Let's go. I'm not actually a fan of hot chocolate. I much prefer your Silver Oak Cabernet Sauvignon."

Hazel took the offered hand. "*I* like hot chocolate," she murmured, confused. Was this friendly hand-holding? Were those friendly sparks, running up her arm and jolting her heart?

"Hear that? *She* likes hot chocolate," the barista called out. "I recommend you make her another cup when you two get home." She straightened and went to her machines, then returned with a small paper package in her hand. "Here. This'll make it easier." She chucked the package across the room at River.

He caught it midair with his free hand. "For crying out loud. Do you always throw cocoa at your customers?"

Grinning, the barista shrugged. "Hey, I'm rooting for you. You two make a cute couple."

"We're just friends." Hazel tried to gently tug her hand from River's. She didn't want to hurt his feelings. But it was definitely too much. Already, the sparks running up her arm had turned into fire. But River held her hand tight and didn't even notice.

"Sure you are," was the last thing Hazel heard from the barista. Then, she and River were back out in the cold harbor. The door to the café clicked shut behind them.

"Never mind the barista, Hazel. Come on." River let go of her hand but only to wrap his arm around Hazel's shoulder instead. It protected her from the rising wind as they hurried toward his car, but it did nothing to extinguish the sparks on her skin.

And the nook of River's arm felt like the safest, warmest, most secure place in the world.

She was in so much trouble.

He let go only to open the car door for her, waited until she was buckled in, and then he handed her the fragrant bakery bag to hold.

For a while, they drove in silence. Hazel stared out of her window into the night, arguing with herself in starts and stops and stutters.

River exhaled a low breath. "Hey."

She turned to him. "Hey."

"I didn't mean to... It's strictly a glass of wine and a movie to pass the time," he murmured. "I'll sleep downstairs. No funny business. Promise."

"No, I know." She blushed. So he felt it too.

"Just friends, Hazel."

"Right." *Wrong.*

"Right." He pulled into the same spot in the little parking lot by the bridge. This time, River didn't put his arm around her shoulder or stop to admire the creek, and by the time they were back upstairs in Hazel's kitchen, she was too cold to wonder about his feelings for her.

While River called his mother to let her know about the missed ferry, Hazel heated milk for the barista's cocoa and poured River another glass of wine. Then she went into her living room, slipped a DVD into the player, and sat on her comfy couch. The fragrant steam rising from her drink smelled of dark chocolate and sweet cream. Hazel wrapped her hands around the warm mug and pulled her feet up.

When River joined her, he frowned. "I was going to make your cocoa."

"I couldn't wait. I'm so cold."

"Still?" He took a blanket from the chair and shook it out. "Here." He wrapped it around her, making sure her feet were tucked under it.

She smiled up at him. "Thank you. Your wine is still in the kitchen."

When he came back with his glass, he sat beside her. "What are we watching?"

"A feel-good movie about women banding together to overcome obstacles." It was Hazel's favorite, and she wanted to see what he thought of it. Smiling, she pressed the play button. "How do you feel about watching something like that?"

He cheered her with his wine. "Beggars can't be choosers. Just kidding. Let's see it."

The movie started, and within the first half hour, a heartbreaking plot twist made Hazel cry. She did her best to keep it together, but finally, a tiny tear stole past her defenses and rolled down her cheek.

Hoping he wouldn't notice, she quickly wiped it away. But soon, a bigger tear followed the first.

Without saying anything, River took her empty mug and put it on the coffee table, then wrapped his arm around her and pulled her to him.

It felt just as safe and secure and sparky as before. Hazel closed her eyes and soon forgot the sad story. But then, without planning to, she suddenly straightened.

He let her go. "What is it?"

Hazel paused the movie. "I'm sorry, River." She cleared her throat. "I'm just...so confused."

He leaned back, running a hand through his hair. "I know." He sighed and closed his eyes. "This is too hard," he murmured under his breath.

Hazel knew what he meant. "This doesn't feel like *friends*. At least not to me."

"It's not." He set his glass beside her mug and stood. "It's not working, Hazel."

"Where are you going?"

He thrust a thumb over his shoulder. "I'd better go downstairs. I can't be sitting next to you when you're so sweet and..." He bit his lip. "I'd better go."

"But..." She put her feet on the ground. "No, don't go."

"*Don't* go?" He dropped his hands.

Hazel took a deep breath. "I didn't say it felt bad. On the contrary. It just doesn't feel like *friends*."

His voice was raw when he spoke. "Then what does it feel like to you, Hazel?"

"It feels like...more."

It was a long time before he spoke. "A month ago, I popped the question to my ex. I wanted to marry her. Have kids, grow old together."

Hazel tilted her head, studying his face. "You still love her."

River rubbed a hand along his jaw. "I don't think I do. It was a shock, certainly. But once I got over the rejection, it felt easy to let her go. Too easy, if I'm being honest. But something in me is waiting for the other shoe to drop. Every morning I wake up, thinking today's the day where it finally catches up with me and I'll be crushed.""You aren't sure whether you're over her." Hazel didn't want to hear about River's ex. But it was only a sign that she was in too deep already. She needed to know how he really felt.

"What I *am* sure of is that I'm attracted to you. More than I should be. More than..." He took a breath as if he was short of air. "I won't be able to keep my hands off you tonight if I stay with you. And I know something else."

"What is that?" Hazel's spine tingled; she no longer wanted him to keep his hands off her. She'd offered friendship to protect her heart. But the way she was built, his touch and friendship weren't compatible. Her desire for River was winning the race.

River gestured between them. "Whatever this is we have? It's more than I'm willing to risk on a rebound."

When his meaning sank in, Hazel exhaled softly. "Okay," she whispered.

His throat moved. He went to stand behind where she sat on the couch, the backrest between them.

Hazel shifted and tilted her head to see his face.

River reached out his hand and tenderly cupped her cheek. Moving slowly, he locked eyes with her and leaned in for a deep, drawn-out kiss. This time, it wasn't just a peck on the forehead, but a full kiss on the lips.

Hazel melted into the warmth of his lips, savoring the taste of wine and yearning for more. There was an unspoken longing and regret between them that filled the air.

"Good night," he whispered, stroking her cheek with his thumb before pulling away.

"Wait!" Hazel's eyes flew open. Was he really leaving after a kiss like that? "Where are you going?"

But River didn't even turn around, already reaching for the doorknob. It was as if he was determined to leave without looking back, afraid that he might change his mind. "I'll sleep in my car," he said, his voice hoarse. "And definitely not anywhere near Lover's Lane."

And then he was gone, his steps echoing down the stairs and out of the store and down the lane, fading away until Hazel could no longer hear them. And just like that, he was gone.

CHAPTER 20

"Have fun exploring the cove's maritime museum, girls." The elderly woman sitting behind the old-fashioned register handed Audrey three yellow paper tickets. She nodded at the wide-open doorway that led into the next room and picked up the crochet hooks waiting in her lap. "No cursing and no chewing gum, and, uh, no..." She scrutinized them over the rim of her reading glasses. "I forget what else. Enjoy."

"Thank you." Smiling, Audrey waved her friends onward. After a week of unbroken sunshine, the morning fog stubbornly lingered on the beaches and golden hills, refusing to dissolve. Low, gray clouds hung like a ceiling over the cove, dampening everyone's spirits. Audrey and Georgie had been arguing all morning about where to place the handicap ramp. Much as Audrey loved her great-aunt, it was a relief to see her friends.

"I really needed to get out." She pulled her tote bag higher on her shoulder and stole a glance at Hazel.

There were pale blue shadows under her eyes.

The night before, River had missed the last ferry back to the cove. This morning, he seemed distant and reserved. Audrey was certain that Hazel was the reason behind his sudden change in demeanor. However, despite her inquisitive questions, River revealed nothing. He had only sat down briefly for breakfast before setting off again to visit another doctor on the island.

All Audrey knew was that the day before, her brother had offered Hazel a ride back to Lover's Lane and that he spent the night in his car after missing the last ferry.

The two of them had driven to the island around eleven. Before *lunch*.

So how had River managed to miss the last boat? Even if he had an outdated schedule on his phone, there should have been plenty of ferries to pick from.

Obviously, he'd been too busy dropping off Hazel to return to the cove. All afternoon, he'd been too busy...

Hazel came to stand beside her, and Audrey pointed at the model of a sailing ship displayed in a glass case. "Pretty, isn't it?"

"Mh-hmm." Hazel nodded in agreement. "Pretty. And big."

"Yeah." Audrey pressed her lips together. She badly wanted to ask Hazel what was going on between her and River. But even though Hazel had joined her, she wasn't looking at Audrey. All morning, she'd avoided eye contact.

"If I'm honest, models bore me to tears," Audrey admitted suddenly, earning herself a quick glance and a smile from her new friend.

"They don't do much for me either." Zoe joined them. "But this room is so lovely I'll even look at the model ships just to spend time in here."

Lovely was the perfect word to describe the charming museum. "It's my first time coming here." Audrey turned to admire the large room they were in. The big windows overlooked the ocean that shimmered like pearl-gray silk in the dull light outside. But inside the museum, the walls were painted the soft blue green of a riverbank in summer. The warm glow of lights made it easy to forget the clouds outside, while the delicate scent of old paper and lemon floor polish softly permeated the air. It was pleasantly warm, and the old wooden floors creaked cozily as Zoe, Audrey, and Hazel made their way from one display to the next.

Glass cases and tables created a path through the space. Many displayed fossils found in the local caves and cliffs, while others showcased maritime artifacts like brass compasses, faded maps, and broken cargo from old shipwrecks that storms had washed ashore.

In one corner stood a large bookshelf filled with books. Audrey assumed they were about the history of the local coastline or the works of local historians. A few comfortable armchairs were arranged nearby, inviting visitors to stay and read for a while.

"Mmh." She nudged Zoe and nodded at the welcoming spot. "I wouldn't mind reading a book over there."

"I know. It's like stepping into the living room of an old sea captain's house, isn't it?"

Together, the three of them walked to the next glass case. "Shark teeth," Zoe announced confidently. "And fossils."

Audrey leaned closer. "The big one there is a fish. Wow." She pointed to the label. "A local family donated it. That's nice."

"It *is* nice. They could have sold it to a big museum. I haven't seen many fish like this." Zoe tilted her head.

Audrey grinned. "How many have you seen?"

Zoe returned the smile. "I'm more of an art museum person. Anyway, there's just one more room left," she said, leading the way. "Perhaps we can grab coffee afterward." Zoe snagged a brochure from a small information booth as they walked by. "It's my last day in the cove, and I could use a little treat before heading back to Seattle."

Audrey glanced at her friend. "How long do you have to stay there before you can come back?"

Zoe shrugged. "I'm already scheduled to work through the next three weekends, though I said I couldn't do weekends this month. I really feel like it's time to start my own business. I'll still work weekends, but at least I'll be doing it for my own pocketbook."

"Did the Brooklyn barista ever ask her dad how much he wants for the café?" Audrey asked.

Zoe sighed. "Whatever it is, I don't have the money. It's a soap dream, and I shouldn't have encouraged that conversation."

"You have to *believe* in your Mendocino bakery," Audrey said. "Maybe it won't happen right now, but sometime, for sure."

"Right. I'll manifest a whole bakery out of sheer air with my positive thoughts and all." The corners of Zoe's lips curved slightly.

"There you go." Audrey wanted nothing more than for her friend to open her own business. Ideally in the cove, but the island would do. Especially once the ferry sorted itself out again. "That's the spirit."

They went through the dark doorway that led into the other room the museum had to offer.

Unlike the spacious first room, this one was small. It could have been a butler's pantry before the original house was converted into a museum.

The pretty overhead light in its ornate ceiling medallion was dimmed. Navy curtains veiled the windows, casting what little sunlight filtered through a mysterious deep-water blue. In the middle of the small room stood a single, large glass case, and a single devoted spotlight illuminated the shimmering contents.

When they saw what it was, Audrey inhaled. "Wow. Look at this. It's a proper treasure."

Zoe pointed to an intricate golden necklace spilling from a wooden chest. "Gorgeous. Do you think it belonged to a pirate? That's how they staged it."

Audrey leaned in closer to read the label. "Maybe it was a pirate. Local lore has it that a Mendocino man, in the early 19th century, enlisted with a pirate crew in Monterey. When he returned to the cove, he hid his booty in a tidal cave for safekeeping. Later, the treasure was discovered by a local woman." She straightened. "Goodness, that was decent of her. I wonder why she didn't keep it for herself. It must be worth a fortune."

"I would have kept a little for myself," Zoe said thoughtfully. "Just enough to buy a bakery. Come to think of it, maybe I should take a page out of the local man's book, become a pirate myself, and steal this lot here."

"You can't be a pirate without a ship. That's sort of the point," Audrey replied reasonably. "Use your head, Zoe."

"Also, this is just a replica and not the actual treasure," Hazel said, smiling. "I think the real deal is in a museum in San Francisco."

"Well, then I'll have to find another way." Zoe sighed. "Maybe I'll check out the remaining local tidal caves."

"No, don't do that, either. They're terribly dangerous," Hazel said. "Whoever the local woman was, she must have been either insane or incredibly brave to do it."

Zoe gazed longingly at a pair of dangling earrings. "I can't even imagine how it would feel to find something like this."

"I know." Hazel leaned closer too. "Look at that dainty ring with the anchor motif. So pretty! I bet a young sailor carried it in his pocket as a surprise for his sweetheart back home." She frowned. "Come to think of it... I'm against pirates. How dare they take away sweetheart rings and hide them in tidal caves? It's simply not right. Some lucky woman could have worn that. Her descendants could *still* be wearing it. What a waste."

"But it's so long ago that it all seems more fairytale than reality, doesn't it?" Zoe chewed on the inside corner of her mouth. "Besides, maybe the woman who found the treasure kept a little something for herself after all. As I see it, she deserved a prize for searching that dangerous tidal cave. Let's hope she took all the prettiest rings and dangly earrings and brought them back into circulation."

"I agree," Audrey said dreamily. "I hope her curiosity and courage were rewarded with a bit of financial freedom."

Hazel chuckled. "I'm not sure how ethical any of this is, but I at least support the wearing of pretty jewelry."

They lingered for a while, thinking about the man who hid the treasure and the woman who discovered it. What had they been like? What drove them to join pirate crews and search dangerous caves? Already they, too, were more fairytale than reality.

"This is definitely the highlight of the museum," Audrey said when she had admired the treasure enough. "And I'm afraid we've seen all there is. Where do we go now? Take the ferry and have a coffee with the Brooklyn barista on the island?"

"The ferry runs only a few times today." Hazel checked the schedule on her phone. "It's at least an hour before the next one."

"I'd love to have an early lunch at the Mermaid Galley before I take off for Seattle, if you're up for it," Zoe said. "On a gray day like this, deer and raccoons are roaming about, jumping out of bushes to cross the road. I prefer to drive while there's enough light to spot them."

"All right, let's go to the Mermaid Galley then," Audrey said. "It's not far. Just down the street and around the corner."

Soon, they were sitting in the upstairs dining room of the rustic restaurant on Main Street. The tables were slowly filling up with locals, but they'd been early enough to snag a table at one of the big windows that looked out over the ocean. Silvery lines of fog weaved over the water like the ghosts of fishing nets cast in the past, and the pale silhouettes of cormorants and gulls dipped in and out of view.

Contentedly, Audrey shrugged out of her jacket. Unlike the bluff outside, the restaurant's dining room was warm and cozy, and it smelled of the savory roast beef, potato dumplings, and red cabbage that was posted as the day's special.

"I know it's early, but I'm going full monty," Audrey declared when Hannah, the Galley's waitress, brought them sweet iced teas. "I'll have the special, please."

"Would you like french fries or potato dumplings?" Hannah put a hand on her hip. "The dumplings are absolutely delicious. And if you pick french fries, I'll never speak to you again. That's how good the dumplings are."

"I'll have the dumplings, please." Obediently, Audrey handed her menu back. There was a chance Hannah was joking, but there also was a good chance she was being serious. It was hard to tell.

"Same for me, Hannah. Thank you." Zoe also handed back her laminated menu.

Hazel followed suit. "I'll stick to clam chowder, please."

"Are you sure, honey pie?" Hannah, who looked like she was only a handful of years older than Hazel, frowned. "The roast is really, really good. The gravy has gingerbread in it, and on a day like this, a nice, thick, mellow gravy can do wonders. It can save your *soul*."

Hazel smiled. "I'm sure it can, but I'd like to stick to a bowl of clam chowder anyway. It's my favorite, and I don't come so often to the cove that I'd miss my chance to taste it."

"If you're sure." Pressing her lips together, Hannah returned to the kitchen.

"Cheers." Smiling, Audrey lifted her glass of sweet iced tea to Hazel. "That was brave, standing up for your meal of choice like that. I'm just glad I wanted the dumplings anyway."

Smiling back, Hazel lifted her glass to the toast. "Cheers! Also to Zoe returning to Mendocino soon. In fact, here's to Zoe returning soon to buy the harbor café. I think a bakery would do better than another café, and much better than a wedding dress store. People only need a wedding dress once in their lifetime, but they want fresh bread every day. And I, personally, would simply love to be able to walk over in the mornings and buy it at your bakery."

"Aww." Zoe clinked her glass. "I'll definitely cheer for that."

"Same. I hope it works out," Audrey joined in, and they started talking about how the bakery might look inside and whether Zoe would keep serving coffee and tea.

Soon, Hannah returned with a basket of oven-hot sourdough bread that smelled good enough to make Audrey's stomach grumble.

"Here you go, girls. That'll keep you alive until your lunch comes." Hannah set the basket in the middle. "And if anyone's opening a bakery...we'd be glad to stop making our own bread." She knocked on the table to underline her words. "So let me know if you do." And with that, she hurried on to the next table.

"There you go. You have customers already." Hazel helped herself to a piece of the crusty, fragrant bread and pulled her hobo bag on her lap. "By the way, I have something I need to show you two."

CHAPTER 21

A udrey bit into her own thick chunk of warm bread. "What do you have to show us, Hazel?" she mumbled, her mouth full of crumbs. Chewing, she craned her neck to peer into Hazel's hobo bag. Her eyes widened in sudden realization, and she swallowed. "Oh! Is it the diary?"

"Yes, it is." Hazel handed Audrey the booklet.

"Thank you." It felt thin and fragile in Audrey's hands, but she was glad to have it back. Carefully, she tucked the diary into her own purse. "You haven't by any chance read it already, have you?" she asked hopefully.

"I couldn't sleep a wink last night." Hazel dug deeper, also pulling out a wad of loose papers before hanging the bag back on the chair. "So yes, I did read it."

"You couldn't sleep either?" Audrey narrowed her eyes.

River had spent the night in his car, and Hazel had been wide awake... What had happened between the two? Had they fought?

Hazel ignored the bait. "I dictated what I read into my computer and printed it out for you." She separated the papers and handed each Audrey and Zoe a stack.

"I'm impressed." Smiling, Zoe took her copy.

Audrey was already scanning the short entries that were separated by dates. "Me too." She looked up. "Thank you so much, Hazel. Was it hard?"

"It was all right once I read myself into it." Hazel smiled. "I've seen both better and worse. But I have to admit that Marianne's hand is pretty bad."

Audrey tilted her head. "Like a...doctor's hand when he's writing prescriptions?"

That caused a small smile to tug on Hazel's lips. "Is there something you'd like to ask me, Audrey?"

"Yes!" Triumphantly, Audrey lowered her diary pages. "I thought you'd never ask! What's going on between you and my brother?"

"Nothing."

"Oh come on. I'm on your side. You can tell me."

Hazel shrugged. "Audrey, seriously. Nothing is going on. Or at least...I don't think so. If something is happening, I don't know what it is. And that's the honest truth."

Zoe was following the exchange. "You and River have a thing?" she asked in a small voice.

"No. Um." Hazel closed her eyes. "We spent yesterday afternoon together. After you two left, River offered me a ride back to the island, and then we took a detour to the lighthouse to meet Dr. Henderson. After that, River grabbed a bite at my place, and then he missed the last ferry because his schedule was outdated. That's all." She opened her eyes again. "Let's talk about the diary, okay?"

"Aw." Zoe's forehead crumpled with disappointment.

Apparently, Audrey's handsome brother was busy breaking hearts left, right, and center. She tapped a finger on the tabletop. "Just one question, Hazel. Did you guys, at any time or under any pretense, kiss each other?"

A faint blush tinged Hazel's skin where her sweater met her neck. "Uh. Maybe."

"*Maybe*? That means you did, didn't you? And here I thought... Now I feel like a complete fool," Zoe complained piteously. "I thought he liked me."

Alarm shaded Hazel's eyes, and a hand flew up to cover her mouth. "Zoe! I had no idea!"

"Never mind. Apparently, it was only *me* who liked *him*." Sighing, Zoe grabbed a piece of bread and fell back in her chair, tearing off a big bite and chewing it with an air of despair. "Why don't men ever like *me*? I mean, why don't the *good* ones like me?"

"There, there. It's only my brother." Audrey patted her friend's hand soothingly. Zoe's heartache couldn't be too serious. She'd only just met River. "I'm sure plenty of good men like you."

"No, they don't. It's only bad ones."

"Come on, now, that can't be right. Anyway, I'm sure it's all a matter of right time, right place." Audrey dabbed her mouth with her napkin and took a long drink of her sweet tea. "I haven't yet managed to find myself a good guy, either."

"I swear I had no idea, Zoe," Hazel mumbled.

"I know. I mean, I don't even *want* a man." Zoe stuffed the last of the bread in her mouth and brushed the crumbs off her hands. "It's just... I really like River's blue eyes."

Hazel frowned, looking guilty.

Audrey laughed. "Never mind, Hazel. Zoe will get over River's blue eyes. Tell me more about what happened last night. I want all the dirty details."

"No," Hazel said decidedly. "There are no dirty details to tell. I want you two to concentrate and read the diary. It's not much; you can finish it before the food comes."

Audrey and Zoe both sat up straight. "Yes, ma'am," Audrey said, surprised Hazel was so firm. Maybe she had caught a case of serious feelings for River. Maybe Hazel didn't really like them joking about River's blue eyes.

Calling herself to order, Audrey lifted her pages and read, her eyes flying over the short sentences. Printed out, Marianne's entries were easy enough to read. It didn't take long to finish.

"Goodness." Audrey laid the paper back on the table. "Poor Marianne! Who did this Robert think he was, telling her how to wear her skirts and her hair? Too bad it's so long ago. I really would have liked a chance to tell him my opinion about his opinion."

"He was very controlling," Hazel said. "Doesn't it sound like everyone expected Marianne to walk, eyes wide open, into an unhappy marriage?"

Frowning, Zoe let her last sheet of paper flutter back onto the table. "The guy sounds awfully like my ex. It was so hard to get out of that relationship. And my parents were cheering me on and supporting me any way they could." She exhaled a tense breath. "Was there more in the diary?"

"That's all we've got." Audrey took out the diary to compare the last sentence of Hazel's copy with the lobster scrawl in the diary. With the help of the printed version, she could decipher the script now too. "It ends with her being spitting mad at Robert for telling her to never interrupt him when he talks."

"Maybe she chucked the diary at him?" Zoe ran her hands through her hair. "I really hope Marianne found a way to save herself."

Hazel took a deep breath. "Me too."

Audrey looked at her friend. "You sound like you know more about Marianne and Robert's story. Do you?"

Hazel rested her elbows on the table, tapping a finger on the papers she had laid out in front of her. "After translating the diary, I decided it was time to finally sift through the stacks of old papers in our family's secretary desk. I swear they've accumulated over several generations."

"And?" Audrey put the diary back into her bag for safekeeping. "What did you find? Anything interesting?"

Hazel nodded. "I found a bundle of letters and notes from my grandmother, *her* mother, and even her grandmother. Reading them, I had an...unfortunate epiphany."

Audrey and Zoe exchanged a glance. "What sort of unfortunate epiphany?" Audrey wanted to know.

"In the diary, Marianne mentioned the name of Robert's mother. Klara. Klara, the dressmaker, who lived on the island." Hazel offered a faint smile. "Klara, who founded the wedding dress store. *My* store."

"Oh. *Oh.*"

"I worked out that Robert would have been my grandmother's brother." Hazel folded her hands. "As far as I know, Grandma never once mentioned him. At least not to me; maybe I was just too young. But Robert would also have been an adult by the time Grandma was born. Clearly, they didn't have much of a relationship."

Audrey bit her lip. She wanted to know more. "You never heard anything at all about him?" she prodded gently.

Hazel shook her head. "The only thing is that I vaguely remember a story about a relative suddenly joining the military. Now I think it must have been Robert. Certainly, the sawmill didn't work out for him."

"Your folks aren't around anymore, are they? Is there anyone you could ask for information?"

"I'm afraid not." Hazel cleared her throat. "My grandmother was a lovely, reserved, quiet person who didn't miss the olden days and never talked about them." Hazel smiled at the memory of her grandmother. "I mostly remember her sitting in the atelier by the window, sewing or sketching while she listened to her shows. I wish I had known to ask about her past. Though I'm not sure she'd have answered."

"I understand. My own grandmother wasn't big on answering questions either. Quite the opposite." Audrey put a thoughtful finger on her chin. "I really would've liked to meet our grandmas. Yours sounds sweet. She sounds like you."

Hazel's smile deepened. "You think I'm *sweet*?"

"I agree with Audrey. You are pretty sweet," Zoe threw in. "I think so too."

"Thanks, I suppose." Hazel played with her bread, and then she sighed. "I'm pretty sure women are supposed to be fierce and independent, not sweet, these days."

"Women can be what they want to be," Audrey said. "They can be sweet. They can be fierce, or weak, or whatever flavor people come in. They can be everything at once."

"Then I'm sweet, I guess, and independent and...broke," Hazel decided.

"I'm definitely not sweet," Audrey said thoughtfully. "I'm competent. Sometimes I'm funny. At least that's what I like to call it." She grinned.

"I'm *sad*." Zoe sighed. "Or rather, lonely. Because cute men don't ever notice me. Only control freaks, like my ex. I bet Robert would have liked me too." She tried to make it sound like a joke, but Audrey heard her voice drop.

"Screw that." Audrey put an arm around her friend and pulled her close. "Men don't define you. You're clever. And artistic. Kinder than you should be. You're marvelous. And you're not lonely because you have me."

"Me too," Hazel said shyly.

"I'm really glad I have you two." Zoe smiled at Hazel. "And I didn't mean to say River shouldn't choose you. I'm happy for you two."

"Thank you for saying that." Hazel smiled back. "Though as far as I know, nobody chose anyone yet."

"Aww. You don't have to play it down on my behalf." With a sigh, Zoe arched her back to stretch.

"You *like* my brother, don't you, Hazel?" River's proposal had failed only a short time ago, and Audrey felt like she should protect her brother from more hurt. It was the sibling code of honor after all...even if River didn't exactly seem to agonize over losing his shot at marriage.

"Of course I *like* him. Who wouldn't? River's wonderful. He's..." Hazel exhaled. "I do like him."

"What *exactly* happened last night between you two?"

"I'd tell you if I knew." Hazel opened her hand, signaling she was done with the topic.

The food arrived on two large plates and a bowl, piping hot and mouthwateringly fragrant. Once the general shuffling of glasses and arranging of silverware was done, they were alone again.

Hazel didn't touch the steaming, creamy chowder in front of her. Instead, she interlaced her fingers. "Let's get back to my old letters. There's more."

Audrey looked up. "What else did you find out?"

"I found a few letters Klara wrote about Marianne."

Audrey almost dropped her fork. "She wrote about Marianne?"

"Yes." Hazel flipped through her notes, pulled a faded letter out, and laid it in the middle of the table. "Here. You can read it."

Audrey put her fork down and wiped her fingers on her napkin before she picked up the yellowing paper.

The hand was elegant and clear. Unlike Marianne's hasty scribbles, Audrey found it easy to read the short staccato sentences Klara had penned in ink.

"What does it say?" Zoe split a soft potato dumpling in quarters and covered one with the rich gravy before putting it into her mouth.

"Klara writes about Mendocino Cove," Audrey murmured, concentrating on the fluid script. "And...here she mentions having tea with Marianne's mother and grandmother. Magda and Phoebe. Magda and *Phoebe*?" Her heartbeat picked up speed. Confused, she put a hand to her throat, pressing the dip between her collarbones as if that would calm it down.

Hazel, who was tasting the clam chowder, lowered her spoon. "Do you recognize the names?"

Audrey nodded. "Phoebe was my family's matriarch. She and her husband came from Nantucket and settled here. Magda was their daughter." She gently placed the timeworn letter on the table and pulled a ballpoint pen from her purse. Then she took a paper napkin and scribbled names and lines on it, outlining a family tree.

There was only one way Marianne could be woven into the tapestry of this family's history.

CHAPTER 22

Audrey opened the front door of the old hotel at Beach and Forgotten and went inside. Hazel followed, her gaze nervously darting around the room.

There was no sign of River. Her eyes flitted toward the sweeping staircase. But the upstairs was as empty as the foyer with its blue-green sea glass chandelier, and Hazel's hope of encountering him faded. "Is your brother home?" she asked Audrey in a hushed voice.

Audrey's eyebrows rose. "He left early for Dr. Henderson's office. Why?"

"Just wondering."

"But why are you wondering?" Audrey smiled and nudged her.

Zoe, who had taken the time to turn the car around, now joined them to say goodbye. "Ladies, it was my pleasure to drop you off here. But if I want to get home before nightfall, I should leave right away. I'll see you again soon." Zoe hugged Audrey, and then she hugged Hazel.

Hazel hugged her back. "Have a good trip back to Seattle."

Audrey nodded. "Quit your job and move here. Or at least don't stay in Seattle so long again."

"Cross your fingers, I guess." Zoe waved, and then she went back outside, closing the door behind her.

"Should we find Aunt Georgie?" Hazel asked once they were alone. "Is she home?"

"I think so." They peeked in the kitchen, but the spacious room was empty, the counters clean and orderly, the stove cold. Audrey led the way through the living room and slid open one of the French doors.

Hazel stepped onto the patio.

Fog sat on the beach like a fluffy hen. The comfortable wicker chairs were deserted, but farther toward the sea, a lone figure sat on a driftwood tree, looking out at the ocean.

"There's Aunt Georgie. Let's go meet her." Audrey kicked off her sandals and started walking.

Hazel also slipped off her ballet flats and stepped barefoot on the beach. The sand still radiated the heat of sunny days, warming the soles of her feet.

"Aunt Georgie?" Audrey called out a warning so they wouldn't emerge from the fog like shadowy ghosts.

Aunt Georgie turned, and when she saw who it was, a smile spread over her face. "I thought you were at the museum."

"We were, and now we are back." Audrey leaned down to kiss her aunt's cheek.

Hazel smiled, remembering how Audrey had teased her brother about kissing people's cheeks. Apparently, he wasn't the only one.

Aunt Georgie looked at Hazel. "Hi, darling. What are you two up to now that you've seen the cove's maritime treasures?"

"We wanted to talk to you about something," Hazel said shyly. She wasn't sure about the older woman's reaction to the news.

Aunt Georgie nestled her back against an old branch. "What about?"

They settled on the weathered trunk on either side of Aunt Georgie. Like the sand, the sun-bleached, dry wood was warm. The sea, as if sending out fog was enough effort for the day, lay still and quiet like molten silver. Close by, a sea lion barked, its call echoing over the tranquil water.

"Do you remember the diary I found in the attic?" Audrey asked.

"Of course I do." Aunt Georgie nodded. "Have you managed to decipher the handwriting? Did you find out anything more?"

"We did." With help from Hazel, Audrey explained what they'd found out about Robert and Marianne.

Aunt Georgie furrowed her brow. "Poor Marianne. But why did my mother call out her name?"

Gently, Audrey took her hand. "Because Marianne was her older sister. Much older, in fact. But Marianne was your aunt."

Aunt Georgie's eyes widened. "My *aunt*? I never heard about an aunt, Marianne or otherwise."

Audrey pulled the napkin from her pocket. "Look at this. We put it together."

Aunt Georgie studied the names and lines and dates. "Goodness," she finally murmured. "Why did Mom never talk about Marianne? What was the big secret?"

Hazel wrapped her arms tighter around herself. This was the part she'd been dreading to tell. She hadn't even shown that letter to Audrey yet. But now it was time. She took a deep breath of the cool, salty air that smelled of dried kelp and sea lion. "The truth is—the wedding never took place. Marianne disappeared."

"Marianne *disappeared*?" Audrey frowned. "You didn't tell me!"

"I'm sorry," Hazel whispered. "I feel so bad about it."

Aunt Georgie's forehead crumpled into inquisitive wrinkles. "Marianne disappeared? But that's good! Then she didn't marry this terrible Robert?"

"It seems like she did not," Hazel confirmed. "His mother was very, very angry with Marianne because of it. She wrote a letter claiming Marianne had run away with another man. A stranger who came through town in search of temporary work at the mills." The letter had ended up in the secretary desk instead of being sent off to a friend. Hazel suspected Klara had decided against venting—and exposing her familiarity with some distinctly unladylike expressions.

"Another *man*?" Aunt Georgie tucked her chin in disbelief. "Now, maybe. But back then, it would have been such a scandal here in the cove. I'm sure I'd have heard *something* about a family member running off with a stranger, never to be seen again." Aunt Georgie shook her head. "Whatever happened, I promise you *that* was not it."

"I agree." Audrey leaned forward. "Marianne wrote nothing in her diary about meeting any strangers, let alone men. Not once."

"I'm with you too." All night, Hazel's mind had mulled over theories of what could have happened. "Marianne struggled with Robert's controlling behavior, not complicated love triangles. I think Klara attacked her good name and character because it was easier to blame Marianne than her beloved son."

Aunt Georgie sighed, her eyes fixed on the horizon. "So Marianne disappeared just like Willow. Is that why Mom called her name on the beach that night?"

"Maybe she was calling for her sister to guide her daughter," Audrey said softly. "No wonder poor Grandma sent you to Nantucket to save you. She really did think the cove was cursed. Her trauma ran even deeper than we realized."

Aunt Georgie frowned. "One way or the other, Mom was a big one for keeping secrets."

Audrey leaned her head on her aunt's shoulder. "It was a different time. I'm sure she did the best she could."

"Well, I can't believe she never once mentioned Marianne to us! What else is in these letters?" Aunt Georgie demanded from Hazel.

Hazel cleared her throat. "Klara accused Marianne of breaking her son's heart and driving him into joining the military. Apparently, he requested to be stationed overseas and left right away."

"Robert left Mendocino the moment his fiancée vanished?" Audrey interlaced her fingers, her eyes worried. "His fiancée who wrote in her diary about his increasingly abusive behavior?"

"It does sound suspicious, doesn't it?" Hazel's heart was heavy with the weight of what might have happened. No wonder her sweet, quiet grandmother had kept Robert's existence shrouded in silence. "I sincerely hope he had nothing to do with Marianne's disappearance."

"Who disappeared?" a deep voice asked.

Hazel wheeled around. "River!" She hadn't heard his footsteps on the sand, but he was already close enough to have overheard her words.

"Hello, darling," Aunt Georgie greeted River, her expression distracted.

Audrey jumped off the log and went to her brother, hugging him. "You're back!"

River embraced his sister and smiled at Hazel, but there was no kiss on the cheek this time. "Who disappeared?"

"Marianne," Audrey filled in. "Her fiancé, Robert, murdered her."

"We don't know that he did," Hazel protested weakly. "I mean, it doesn't look good, but—"

"*Murdered?* Who is Robert?" River blinked, trying to understand what he had walked into.

"It all happened a long time ago," Audrey said quickly. "I'll catch you up later. How did it go with Dr. Henderson?"

"Good. Busy. He's leaving tomorrow." River rolled up his sleeves, clearly too warm despite the fog that rolled over the beach. The gray merino sweater was a great fit for his style and physique, but Hazel tried not to stare. "I'm only here to change and grab a few things. I still have to make a patient visit on the island."

"Oh, then you won't mind bringing Hazel home again." Audrey grinned widely. "Zoe drove us here, but she's left now, and Mom took my car."

Hazel stifled a groan at her friend's request. River looked at Hazel as if he'd heard it, and a smile appeared on his lips. It was genuine but crooked, tugging more on one corner of his mouth than the other.

"It's not necessary—" Hazel started.

"May I offer you another ride to the island?" he asked.

"I can walk if you're in a hurry," Hazel said weakly. "Look." She pointed to her feet, remembering too late she was barefoot. "I mean to say, I'm not wearing heels today. I can just walk. I walk all the time."

River's lips moved as if he wanted to comment on her bare feet, or maybe the fact that she walked all the time, or possibly that they'd been here before. But in the end, all he said was, "I'm driving anyway. You might as well catch a ride."

"Okay. Thanks," Hazel said, feeling small. It suddenly seemed like a poor judgment call to come to River's house the day after he'd decided to drop whatever was between them.

"Exactly, he's driving over there anyway," Audrey said happily, and even Aunt Georgie nodded her approval and said, "Of course he's taking you back with him, darling. You don't want to walk that far, especially on a foggy day like this. You'll step off the bluff because you can't see the edge. Then what?"

Hazel had never heard of anyone stepping off the bluff because it was foggy, but she let it go and only nodded meekly.

River checked the watch on his wrist. "Well, I have what I need from the house. I only came out here because I was wondering why you're all sitting on the beach in this weather. But I should get going now."

"That's fine. I have to start our seafood paella for dinner and pour Aunt Georgie a stiff drink," Audrey said busily. "Hazel, we'll meet again soon. Keep digging around those old papers in your secretary desk. Maybe you can find out more about what happened."

Hazel exhaled. "Okay."

"Great." River had already turned back to the house. "Don't wait for me with dinner if I'm late, Audrey. I'll grab something when I get back."

She smiled, tilting her head. "Yes, do take your time. I'll put a plate in the fridge for you."

"Here." Hazel handed Aunt Georgie Klara's letters. "I think you should have these."

Aunt Georgie accepted the folded paper with a grateful nod. "I would like to read them," she admitted. "I promise to return them to you, darling."

"Thank you." Hazel smiled, glad Aunt Georgie now knew that Hazel's family was entangled with Marianne's disappearance, and relieved she didn't seem angry about it.

"You'd best catch up with River," Audrey said, making a shooing motion with her hands.

"I'll be back soon." Hazel waved before hurrying after her ride.

She finally caught up to him on the patio, where he sat in one of the wide wicker chairs, brushing the sand off his feet.

Hazel followed his example and stepped back into her ballet flats. When she looked up, she saw that he was watching her with a smile in his blue eyes.

CHAPTER 23

For a moment, the cawing of the gulls above faded to white noise in Hazel's ears. No matter what feelings River had decided to drop, when his blue eyes looked at her like that... Hazel's smile wavered for a moment, a subtle tension lingering in the corners of her eyes. Was it just her, or did a mixture of hope and apprehension hang in the air?

She blinked, trying to relieve the tension. "Hey, River."

"Hey, Hazel."

"How are you?"

"Fine. Well, in all honesty, I didn't get much sleep last night." He ran a hand through his hair. "And I wanted to say—I'm sorry I behaved the way I did. I shouldn't have gone back to your place when I already knew... I apologize for causing all that confusion." His smile left his lips. "And I'm glad to see you. I meant to talk to you as soon as possible."

"Oh. There's no need to apologize, River. I practically made you come back to my place. I also could've..." She took a deep breath. "What I mean to say is that I caused just as much confusion."

"You *made* me? Twisted my arm and marched me up Lover's Lane, did you?" His smile deepened.

"Sort of. Reheated lasagna, you know? Who among us can resist that siren song?"

"Ah, siren song. Yeah, there was a bit of a siren song involved, I believe." River stopped talking abruptly.

Hazel suddenly felt like rolling up her own sleeves to cool down. It was as if River controlled the switch to her internal thermostat. "Well, anyway. It was all just the wine talking." It was only the wine *kissing*, more like.

They went into the house, quickly passing through the rooms and out the front. "One glass?" River closed the door behind him and pulled out the key fob to unlock his car. "No, it wasn't the wine. Not for me." His voice had changed, becoming softer and deeper.

"Um. River?" Hazel stopped by the passenger door. She wasn't ready to continue this conversation. Not now.

"Yeah?"

"Let's not try to figure this out. Sometime soon. But not right now." Hazel smiled an apology. "I think I need a day or two to let things settle."

"Of course. You're right." He opened her door and closed it behind her, then went to sit in the driver seat.

"Oops. Sorry. I didn't see that."

River leaned over and picked up the empty paper coffee cup that rolled by her feet, tossing it into the back. "Sorry about the mess, Hazel. I'm not usually messy."

Hazel closed her eyes, trying not to breathe in his scent. But it was impossible to avoid. He was too close, and an intoxicating blend of masculine body wash, freshly brewed coffee, and his own heady sandalwood essence washed over her, sweeping her up as easily as an ocean wave.

"Hazel? Are you dizzy?"

She opened her eyes. "Yes. Yes, I am a little dizzy. Never mind, though. I'll breathe through it."

He reached out and took her wrist. Before she understood what he was doing, he had his thumb on her pulse and was checking his watch, counting silently.

His touch did nothing to heal her dizziness.

"Are you upset with me?" He let go of her wrist. "Your pulse is really fast."

She circled her wrist protectively with her other hand. The spot where his fingers had pressed into her skin felt like it glowed brightly, the source of an invisible current that ran up her arm. "River, I'm *fine*," she managed to get out. "Stop taking my pulse like that, please."

"Like how?"

"Like... Let's... How is Dr. Henderson?"

A line appeared between River's eyes. "If you're dizzy, maybe you should lie down. There are plenty of empty bedrooms in this house."

"No! Uh. I was just kidding." She blinked. The last thing she should do was spend the night in his house and muddy the waters of her heart even more. "I'm fine. I promise." His concerned look softened her lips into a smile. "I promise," she said again, more softly. "If I'm upset, it's over something that happened a long time ago. That's all. I really, really don't need to lie down."

"You're upset? Audrey would be more than happy to make you a cup of tea and—"

She fell back in her seat. Half of her wanted to laugh, while the other half wanted to cry. Briefly, she touched his arm. "I just want to go home, River."

It took him a beat or two before he replied. "Sure." The car hummed to life, and he pulled out of the driveway onto Forgotten Lane.

"So," Hazel said, hopeful she'd get a normal conversation going yet. "How *is* Dr. Henderson?"

River checked the traffic and merged, turning toward the ferry. "Good, apart from the hearing. He's going to see a specialist in San Francisco for a cochlear implant. It will take him some time to get used to it. After the surgery, there is a learning process as the brain begins to interpret the signals the implant sends."

"That sounds difficult."

"Yes." River glanced at her. "But he's looking forward to the challenge. All he needs is time to take care of himself."

"It's lucky you came along then. You can stay for a while, can't you?"

He nodded. "I have to admit that the timing worked out just so for both of us."

"For the people on the island, too. I'm glad we have you to stand in for our good doctor."

He gave her a searching glance. "You are?"

"Of course." She smiled sweetly. "Beats sitting around the hospital's waiting room for hours on end."

"Ah." He chuckled. "That sort of glad. Got it."

Hazel rolled down her window so she wasn't tempted to touch his arm again. The slipstream weaved its way into the car, bringing with it the fragrance of forest and ferns and moss. The earthy scents grounded her. "So, where are you going? Who is your patient on the island?"

"Oh, I'm not sure I should kiss and tell, since you're all neighbors." He grinned.

Almost, she laughed. River really was brand-new to the island, and she couldn't resist teasing him. "Nice try, doc, but I'll hear about it at the farmers market anyway. Probably earlier. We islanders tend to catch each other up."

The corners of his lips twitched. "Dr. Henderson warned me about this."

"Did he also tell you that resistance is futile?"

Now, River broke into a grin. "He mentioned it. All right, I'll tell you. It's Mrs. Borden."

"Oh, because of her knee. Yes, she said it was acting up again. It's rheumatoid arthritis. The cool weather aggravated it last year too."

He shook his head. "You already know more than I do then."

Hazel rolled up her window and brushed a strand of hair back behind her ear. "Let me tell you how it works on the island. The cove too, by the way."

He laughed. "Please do."

She took a breath and told River what she knew about life in Mendocino, and River paid back the favor with stories from his residency.

Anecdote followed anecdote, and even though the ferry was late again, when River drove off the boat and onto the island, it felt like no time had passed at all.

They were driving up Harbor Street when his phone rang. He answered, letting the caller know they were on speaker phone and that there was another passenger in the car.

"Who is the other passenger?"

Hazel easily recognized Mrs. Borden's voice. "Hi, Helen," she called out. "It's me, Hazel."

"Hazel, sweetheart. How are you?"

"I'm fine. Please go ahead and talk to the doctor. I won't bug you."

"You couldn't bug me if you tried. In fact...Hazel, is he on his way to my house?"

"Yes, I am," River answered.

"Would you mind bringing Hazel with you then? I need a hand with...with a personal matter."

"Of course, I'm happy to help out." Hazel glanced out the window. "We'll be there in five minutes, Helen."

"You're heaven sent, sweetheart. Um. So are you, doc. It's just... I don't know you, and my daughter isn't here today. I just need a quick hand, and I'd rather it'd be Hazel. I've known her all her life, you know?"

"Are you okay with this?" River mouthed at Hazel, and she smiled and nodded.

"I've helped Helen plenty of times before," she whispered. "It's fine." She turned back to the dash. "We'll see you in a moment," she promised. "Are you all right until then?"

"I am, knowing that you are coming, sweetheart. I'm in the bedroom, if you could come up and meet me there." Hazel agreed, and the old lady ended the call.

"You've done this before?" River asked. "Do you know what she needs help with?"

"I think she probably needs help getting dressed, or maybe she needs help getting to the bathroom. Whatever it is, don't worry. I took care of my mother when she got sick."

"You did?" He frowned. "Can I ask?"

Hazel looked down at her hands. "In the end, several things came together."

"That's tough."

Hazel nodded. "I miss Mom." She smiled weakly. What wouldn't she do for a word of motherly advice? Not to mention being lonely... "I know I'm being selfish," she admitted sheepishly. "But it's no good, walking this walk without a mother."

"Your mom had you late?"

"She did. Both Grandma and Mom had kids later in life." She looked out of the window. "If I had a choice in the matter, I'd have my kids while I'm still young."

River chewed on his lip. "Is that what you want?" he asked after a while. "Have children soon?"

Something in his voice flipped her thermostat switch again. How did he do it? An inflection in his voice, the searching glance, the way his hand moved as if to take hers, only to land on the gearshift?

"Um. Yes," Hazel admitted, keeping herself from fanning her face with her hand. "If I can, I want to be young with my kids. I want to watch them grow up, and I want to be there for them as long as possible. But, you know..." She let the sentence trail off. The timing wasn't just up to her, after all. Her last boyfriend had been allergic to children. Obviously, it all depended on—

"Me too," River interjected, his voice deep and quiet like a lake in the woods. "I want kids sooner rather than later too. And I'd love to have several, so they'll always have siblings to look out for them." He looked over, his blue eyes catching hers for a moment before he turned back to the road. "My dad left us too soon as well. Mom was struggling to keep the ship afloat, but Audrey was always there for me. Lots of late-night calls. You can tell siblings things you don't necessarily want to put on a parent."

"I think I understand. I can't imagine how it would be to have a sibling. But having a sister sounds like heaven."

"Audrey is the best sister." Again he glanced at Hazel, and the flames inside her flickered and danced, blushing her cheeks and making her eyes widen. Were they really talking about having kids? The look he'd just given her... This was not just casual chatter. Even without a mother's advice, Hazel was woman enough to honor the small insights her intuition threw her way.

For the short remainder of the drive, she studiously avoided looking at the handsome doctor beside her who wanted kids soon and liked to help people, freely kissed her on the cheek, forehead, and lips, and also, explicitly, was just a friend on the rebound.

CHAPTER 24
The Past

M arianne glanced over her shoulder before she opened her diary and dipped her pen into the ink.

It was like that now.

She was constantly looking over her shoulder, even in the privacy of her own room. Robert was so terribly interested in even the smallest details of everything she did that it had become quite an obsession with him. Even Mama had stopped saying it was a sign of his devotion.

The day before, when he had pointed out that the hem of Marianne's skirt was dirty, Mama had frowned, pinched her lips together, and nodded at Grandmama. In turn, Grandmama had raised her mother-of-pearl lorgnette to study Robert.

At first, Marianne had thought it was because of the stupid hem. After all, she *had* kneeled on the sand to inspect some rocks. A few of them looked promising, and, trying to free the fossils inside, Marianne had forgotten the time. When Mama called for her to come inside and greet their guests, she'd only managed a quick brush-off. Apparently, too much sand and too many wrinkles had escaped her attention. In her hurry, she had thought nothing of it. After all, her family was used to it.

But not Robert. The dirty hem had bothered him to a surprising and uncomfortable degree. Surprising, because he lived on an island that was surrounded by beaches. Uncomfortable, because he was angry at her carelessness.

When Robert was angry, he punished Marianne with glares as hard and shiny as polished steel and a silence so stony it made her doubt even her rock chisel could split it. It also made her doubt his love for her.

In fact, as it stood between her and Robert, Marianne doubted a lot of things.

A shiver trickled down her spine, hitting each vertebra with icy dread.

Marianne took a breath that strained her corset and moved her pen from her right hand to the left. She would not be cowed by steely glares and sullen silences. Robert was on the island now. And she was in the cove, safe in her cozy room, with a warm fire flickering in the fireplace. She was free to confide her thoughts to her diary.

Pulling her shawl tighter, she started to write, her weaker hand obscuring the words on purpose. If Mama found the diary, she'd never be able to read it.

Someone followed me again into the cliffs, Marianne scrawled on the paper. *A watcher, cloaked in black, tailing me. I went into a cave that wasn't marked on the map and slipped away while he climbed down the cliff. For a while, I watched him watch the cave as he waited for me. What would he have done had he caught me? I no longer feel safe. For the first time in my life, I'm scared of being alone. I'm young, but it feels as if my time is running out.*

She dipped her pen again.

Anger made me reckless. Knowing my watcher was busy guarding the wrong cave and aware that the tide was leaving, I finally braved the seaweed. I put on the hobnail boots Henry gave me as a birthday gift and scrambled, slid, and waded my way into the treasure cave. For once, instead of being scolded, I was reward-ed. I was rewarded beyond measure.

Marianne paused. The memory of what she discovered, hidden in a deep recess behind a stone ledge at the back of the cave, still caught her breath. The treasure had been shielded by the push of the tide and a barrier of rocks encrusted with barnacles, sharp and pointed like unsheathed swords and drawn daggers.

Again, Marianne leaned over her diary.

If I had a choice, I would not steal from a pirate's stash. But I need money, and this time, I cannot very well ask Mama.

Marianne's lip quivered. She bit down hard, sure that it was not her imagination spooking her. She needed to leave. She needed to get away from the steely glares and the armed silences and the black-cloaked watcher.

She dipped her pen.

Bruised and scraped and exhausted, I rested until the rising tide drove me back to the beach. A wave

almost pulled me into the sea again. At the last mo-
ment, I managed to grab hold and scramble my way
onto a slippery rock.

I survived. So far, I have survived.

Marianne laid down her pen and blotted the paper. For a long time, she sat quietly, her hands in her lap, her eyes closed.

The familiar noises of the house settling for the night and the sweet sea breeze coming from the open window curled around Marianne like purring cats.

A tear stole from her eye and rolled, warm and salty as the ocean, down her cheek. She would miss all this.

Marianne blinked, wiped away the useless tear, and picked up the pen one more time.

Robert won't let me break off our engagement. If he
can't get the treasure, at least he wants my dowry.
I know I should confide in Mama. She is growing
impatient with Robert, and so is Grandmama. But if
they don't side with me after all, I am lost.

Marianne's head hurt. Thinking, she massaged her temple before continuing.

I will go to Mayville tomorrow and find a pawn
shop. I'll say the ring was left to me by a distant aunt
who married a sailor. I'll go under the pretense of
buying a hat, slip away, and leave poor Tessie to find
her own way back.

Marianne stopped and sat back, chewing on her pen. It wasn't exactly *easy* to give poor Tessie the slip. She had helped Marianne out of too many scraps not to know her tricks, and Tessie's expectations of Marianne's behavior were...not high. Pretty low, in fact.

Marianne ripped out the page she'd just covered in words. Then she lit the corner on her candle and dropped the burning paper on a plate. It wasn't the first page Marianne had burned. Her writing had served its purpose. Her feelings and thoughts had come into focus.

She sighed. It was so much easier to climb steep cliffs, brave crushing waves, and suffer barnacle cuts than run away.

Marianne put the pen in the holder, rose, and closed her diary. Moving softly, she blew out the candle and went to the window.

A full moon lit up the night. Careful not to miss anything, Marianne scanned the beach.

A black shadow skulked near the rocks to the far left, pressed into the cliff.

A sea lion—or the watcher.

Marianne quietly stepped back and pulled the wooden shutters closed, shut the glass panes, and dropped the curtains.

In the morning, Robert had a meeting at the sawmill.

That's when she had to manage the trip to the pawn shop on the far side of the train station. An area where no real lady ever went.

But ladies also didn't scamper around cliffs and caves. Marianne had plenty of practice in going where she wasn't supposed to be.

Only the silver moon watched as she slipped the small handful of stolen pirate jewels into the pocket of her dress and pulled her carpet bag from the chest. If Mama asked why she took the bag, Marianne would claim it was to carry back the new hat. Or something. She would think it up when—and if—the question came.

Something moved; a floorboard creaked.

Maybe it was just the cold of the night, warping the wood. But Tessie had a habit of ghosting the corridors at night, making sure everyone was where they were supposed to be. Marianne in particular.

The bag was ready, packed a week ago. She checked the contents once more. It was all there.

Now she had to wait.

Marianne lay in her four-poster. Eyes wide open, she waited until dawn sent the first rays through the shuttered windows, suffusing the silver tapestry of night with her rose-golden smile. By the time she heard Tessie descend the stairs on the way to the kitchen, humming a little tune, Marianne could bear it no longer.

It would have been better if she had managed to sleep; she needed to keep her wits about her. She rose, smoothed her dress, and splashed cold water on her face to chase away any lingering fatigue. When she was done, she pulled out the suitcase from the closet. It already held a portion of the trousseau destined for Robert's house—monogrammed table linens, towels, and a pair of half-knitted oven mitts she had abandoned. Marianne tiptoed to her desk to fetch the slim dagger Grandmama had given her last Christmas to open letters.

Silently, Marianne slid the sharp edge of her dagger along the suitcase lining, creating a cut just long enough to slip in the diary. For a moment, she considered sewing the slit shut again. But her basket was downstairs, and it was already good enough. Her clumsy stitches might be more conspicuous than the clean cut. Besides, looking for her, nobody would think of opening the trousseau suitcase, let alone check the lining.

As quietly as she could, Marianne dragged the suitcase back into the closet and shut the door. Then she put the dagger on top of the spare dress in her carpet bag and went about the business of pinning her hair.

A light knock told her that breakfast was waiting. "Marianne? Are you awake?"

Marianne closed her eyes. She had expected Tessie, not her mother.

"Darling?"

"Yes, Mama. I am doing my hair."

Instead of leaving, Mama opened the door and came into the room. "You look lovely."

Marianne laid down her brush and rose from her chair to face her mother. "I would like to go to Mayville. Today. I would like to..." Her lie whisked the breath from her lungs, but she squared her shoulders and soldiered on, stumbling over the words. "I would like to buy a new hat. *Dress*. I'd like to buy a new dress."

Hats came in hat boxes. She'd not need a carpet bag to bring back a hat.

Her mother's eyebrows lifted in surprise. "*Another* dress? But you have so many new ones already, what with the wedding being so close."

"Yes. But I need one for, uh, for a...for a ball." Marianne pressed her lips tight, groaning inside at herself. What a poor lie that was! The good people of Mendocino Cove had never given a single ball that required a special dress. Ever. The town was too small and remote for grand affairs.

"A *ball?*"

"I mean a *dance*," Marianne said quickly. "I don't know why I said ball. I meant a dance, of course. A dress for a dance. With lots of...lace?"

"But it's October, darling. There is no reason to expect anyone to host a dance now. And you don't even *like* lace."

"I'm sure there will be a Christmas ball." Panicking, Marianne tripped over the words she threw in her own way like so many obstacles. "I mean, a Christmas *dance*."

Now her mother looked worried. "You have plenty of dresses good for a dance. I hardly think..."

"Or maybe I should take up horse riding. Yes. I'd like a riding dress."

Mama stared at Marianne, nonplussed. "A riding dress with lace, darling? And what horse are you going to ride, exactly?"

Right. Robert didn't own a horse.

Marianne exhaled a long breath. "Mama, I just want to go to Mayville," she said miserably. "I need a change of scenery. May I please go? I will ask Tessie to come."

Mama glanced at the packed carpet bag by the dresser. "Marianne, be a good girl and forget about Mayville. I want you to have breakfast with me and Grandmama. We have to tell you some things about...um. Uh. Marriage." She frowned as if they were unpleasant things.

Marianne's eyelids flew open in alarm. Her married friends had already warned Marianne of these motherly talks about wedded life.

"I'm not hungry," she said, hastily grabbing her brush again and plopping down on the chair so her mother wouldn't see her blush. "I'm not ready to come downstairs."

"When have you ever fussed over your hair, darling? It was windswept the day you were born." Calmly, her mother reached out and took the brush from Marianne's hand. "Have I raised a daughter or a coward?"

Marianne lowered her head.

"Christmas ball, my foot." Mama set the brush down, pushed the carpet bag under the bed with her foot, and took Marianne's hand firmly into her own, forcing her to rise. "Your grandmother Phoebe and I *must* talk to you. Today. Now. It can't wait. Come along, darling."

CHAPTER 25

J on lifted his wineglass and clinked his spoon against
the rim.

Expectantly, Hazel looked up, raising her glass to the
toast together with the other guests. The sinking sun of
a gorgeous October evening broke its last fiery rays on
the crystal, scattering dancing spots of rainbow light on
the roof of the vineyard's dining terrace and the guests.

The vintner cleared his throat. "Thank you all for
coming. You're here every day anyway, but..." Jon gave
everyone a few moments to chuckle and laugh and call
out, *hear, hear* before he continued.

"But tonight is special." He turned to Jenny, who was
sitting at his side. She looked up at him, her blue eyes
smiling. "My beautiful Jenny and I are so happy we...
I... *Erm.*" His throat moved. "In short, we're here to
celebrate the fact that, as of yesterday, our new house
has a roof!"

Everyone cheered and called out, and someone even
whistled.

Grinning, Jon held up his hands. "I know. It's been
a trip. My hair has definitely got a lot grayer since
we started building. But you all have heard more

than enough about the house. The fireplace. The steel beam? The *balcony*? Can you even believe what happened to the balcony?" His laugh was answered tenfold by his guests. Hazel smiled. The balcony had turned out fine after all. She'd not heard the details from the family. But in the roundabout way of small towns, the stories had made their way to her as well.

Jon lowered his hands, calming the laughter and most of the chatting. "Listen, that's all over and dealt with." His face quieted, and he raised his head, looking straight at his family and friends. "What I really want to say is...you made sure Jenny and I got through it all. The sense of belonging that you've gifted us is much more important to this home than the bricks that form its walls. When Jenny and I look at our new house, we see not just our new home, but a testament to the power of unity, friendship, and family."

He cleared his throat. The guests, sensing a change in his mood, stopped moving and fell silent. He lifted his glass higher.

"May the doors of this house always be open, may we together create many cherished moments within the walls, and may the bonds of our friendship never waver. Cheers to family, friends, and a home filled with love." Jon's lips moved, but no other words came. Then he chuckled and put a tender hand on Jenny's shoulder. "Sorry. I love you all. And I love this woman. Always have, always will. That's all. I don't even care about the roof and the balcony as long as I have that."

Smiling, Jenny put her hand on his. "Same," she mouthed, but the sound was drowned by the couple's cheering friends.

The warm night air was filled with love, wrapping around Hazel like a mother's comforting hug. It wasn't just the obvious affection of the engaged couple but also the love of family and the steadfast, kind friends who saw goodness in one another and held on through the highs and lows of human relationships.

The cheers and clinking of wine glasses faded back into the normal chatter of a festive crowd sampling their appetizers, and Hazel relaxed back into her chair. She glanced at the woman who had invited her.

Jenny's blonde, shoulder-length hair was twisted in a low knot. She wore a linen dress that complimented her tan and simple gold jewelry that glinted in the light of the lanterns. As always, Jenny looked elegant, understated, and beautiful.

Hazel hoped against all odds that Jenny was going to love the inexpensive wedding gown she had ordered online.

"Dinner's here! Watch out, everybody! Hot, hot, hot!" Hannah arrived with a posse of teenage waiters, all carrying dinner plates the size of wagon wheels.

"Thank you." Hazel smiled at the boy who slid a plate of portobello risotto in front of her. He nodded and moved on.

"Hey, Hazel."

Hazel's heart hiccuped. She looked to her right. "Hey, River."

He had arrived late, slipping into the empty chair beside her after the toasts had started.

She took a deep breath of the air that was fragrant with the delicious scents of dinner. "Long time no see, stranger."

"I know. I'm sorry." River shook out his napkin. "I've been busy at Dr. Henderson's praxis. I only made it to dinner because most of my patients came as well." He smiled at her with the blue eyes of his mother. "But I'm sure glad I did. I'm starving."

Everyone had been served and started eating. Haze picked up her silverware. "How is your new job going then?"

"It's good. Great, in fact. People miss Dr. Henderson, but they are very welcoming nevertheless." River tasted his steak. "Oh." He took another bite and closed his eyes, chewing. "This is the best food I've ever had in my life."

"Yeah?" Hazel smiled. "I'm glad. I'm also very glad that you feel welcomed." Naturally, she had heard the island's opinion of the new doctor. A little young in most people's opinion, but he seemed to know what he was doing. He listened, took his time, and had good bedside manners. The verdict was that all in all, if they couldn't have Dr. Henderson, the new doctor would do very nicely.

River nodded. "I like my new patients. And I think they like me too."

"Is that right?" Smiling, Hazel took a sip of her white wine. The grapes had grown in this vineyard, and while

Hazel knew nothing about wines, the golden liquid was cool and sweet and maybe the best she'd ever tasted. "How do you know your patients like you, River?"

He winked at her. "It's the little things. Everyone seems to know my name. And they smile when I come into the room. They smile like I'm an old friend. Sometimes, they even do as I say to get better." River shook his head in wonder. "After working at big hospitals, trust me when I say that I appreciate it." He sat back and lifted his glass, sampling the red wine that had come with his own entrée before setting it back down. Then he smiled. "I wonder..."

Already, the familiar warmth of his presence tingled in her cheeks. "What do you wonder?"

He leaned closer. "I wonder if one of the locals put in a good word for me?"

Smiling, Hazel met his eyes. It hadn't taken much. Her neighbors were curious about the young man standing in for their beloved doctor. It had been the talk of the farmers market and the ferries, the grocery aisles and small stores on Lovers Lane.

Apparently, the entire island had seen Hazel and River walking up Lover's Lane together at night, disappearing into her house. Of course they came to ask her what he was like.

Unaware of all the nosy questions and suggestive comments Hazel had fended off, River put his glass back down. "I *knew* it was you. Thank you, my dear. You've made my first work experience very special. I'll always remember it."

"I didn't do anything, River. Merely answered some questions." She smiled, glancing at him. "Fine. Maybe it was a lot of questions. Anyone would have done the same."

He smiled back at her. "That's exactly what I mean. You don't even notice how kind you are." He looked out at the colorful vineyard spreading below them, set ablaze by the sunset. "I've only been here for a short time. But somehow, I feel at home in Mendocino."

Hazel wanted to touch his arm, or even better, run her hand up his neck and curl her fingers into his dark hair. But of course, that was impossible.

Already, Audrey was glancing at them too often from across the table, clearly curious about their conversation.

And River was still working through his last relationship. As he'd said, attraction was just part of the puzzle. Necessary, but not enough for Hazel.

If she felt more than he did, if she was more secure knowing what she wanted than he was—that was on her.

Without realizing it, she had followed his example and leaned closer to him. Their heads were almost touching.

"I'm glad," she said, pulling back. "How is your wine?"

For a moment, River held her gaze. "Everything's better when you are around," he murmured finally. "Hazel, I've really been looking forward to seeing you. I wonder..."

She took a bite, willing the warmth spreading inside her body to at least not show on her face. "What do you wonder, River?"

"I wonder whether I can bring you home again tonight," he said so softly only Hazel could hear the words. "Say yes, please. It's been a whole week. I...miss you."

"I'd like that," she whispered back. Maybe they were talking too quietly for people to hear. But besides Audrey, several other guests had begun to glance over at them, curiosity in their eyes. "Let's eat, River. Everyone is looking at us."

He picked up his knife and fork again. "Eating won't help. They don't look because they're curious but because you're so beautiful."

"Oh...um. Thanks." Smiling, she shook her head at him, and then she focused on her dinner and the man sitting at her other side, who turned out to be Faye's fiancé, a detective named Gabe.

Hazel and Gabe chatted about the grapes, the fog, and the baby who was to come.

But all the while, River's voice echoed in her ear.

Say yes, please. I miss you.

She missed him too. It had only been a week since they saw each other. But for every one of those days in between, Hazel missed River with every fiber in her being. She missed him unreasonably, fervently, with an ache that grew each passing day.

She had tried her best to stop thinking of him. After all, they'd only just met, and it made no sense that she should have feelings for him, let alone intense ones. But her attempts didn't work. In fact, they backfired on her. The more she tried not to think of River, the more she did, and once or twice, he even invaded her dreams... All in all, instead of forgetting him, Hazel now felt like she'd missed River all her life.

No matter what her brain said, feelings didn't always seem to make sense. Instead, they sprouted and grew without encouragement, twisting their greening vines around thoughts and routines and the long, solitary hours Hazel spent in her store, waiting for brides in search of a wedding dress.

Dessert came long before Hazel made much of a dent into the delicious food on her plate. She gladly let the risotto go even though it was delicious, rich and savory and creamy. But butterflies and creamy rice simply didn't mix, nor did the hot apple tarts topped with vanilla ice cream, glazed walnuts, and smooth caramel sauce. Usually, she'd eat every last crumb. Now, Hazel managed only a few bites before the fluttering in her stomach won out.

I miss you.

She glanced at River, glad he was too busy tackling his own dinner to notice her lack of appetite. Otherwise, he might have gone for her pulse again. And Hazel didn't need her heart racing any harder than it did.

She turned away from River and caught the eye of the detective, Gabe. He smiled indulgently at her, as if he knew exactly how she felt.

When the music started, Jon and Jenny rose hand in hand, calling for their guests to join them on the dance floor.

Smiling, Hazel turned in her chair to watch Jon lead Jenny to the center of the roofed terrace. They both looked so happy and in love; it made her heart sing.

More couples soon followed the hosts, and as they started dancing, the last light of the warm, golden day vanished behind the blazing hills. The lanterns glowed brighter in the falling dark, and a myriad of string lights flickered to life in the old oak beams above, twinkling as bright and incandescent as stars in the clear night.

Finished with his dessert, River also turned to watch the dancers, resting an elbow on the back of his chair. "It's still strange for me to see my mother like this."

"Because of your dad?" Hazel asked softly.

"Because she's so in love." He sighed. "It's like she's a whole new person. Happier than she was before, even when Dad was still alive. She wasn't unhappy; she's not the type to be unhappy. She just wasn't—like *that*." Smiling, he nodded at his mother, who was laughing at something a friend had called out as she and her partner swirled past.

"How do you feel about that?" Was it hard for River to see his mother so in love, glowing in the arms of a man who wasn't his father?

He turned to her, his blue eyes clear. "Honestly? I'm glad. I'm relieved Mendocino Cove welcomed her with open arms. She found a home and a community when she needed it most."

"And Jon?" Hazel smiled. "How do you feel about the wedding?"

River put his chin on the arm that rested on the back of the chair, studying her face. Then he smiled back. "Jon couldn't be a better man, and from what everybody tells me, he's waited all his life for her. What else can a son ask for? I'm happy that they found each other." He paused before straightening his back again. "Mom went through a lot. She deserves a new beginning. She deserves true love." He looked at Hazel. "We all do."

Intuitively, Hazel reached over to touch his arm. "You are a good man, River."

River tucked an escaped curl behind her ear, letting his fingers linger. "Not nearly as good as I should be, I'm afraid. Have I told you already that you look gorgeous?"

The flutter moved from Hazel's stomach to her heart, making it hard to breathe. She shook her head. "You said I was beautiful. Gorgeous, you forgot to mention."

"I didn't forget. I've been whispering the words in my head on a loop. It feels like I've been telling you all night." He let his finger trail down her jaw, his touch burning a bright path on her skin. "You are everything to me, Hazel," he murmured. "You are the stars, the moon, the sea on a summer day."

"Yeah?"

"Yeah."

Hazel inhaled what air she could. It wasn't much, maybe only enough to fill a thimble, but it made it possible to say a few breathless words. "What are you going to do about it, River?"

He smiled and cupped her face, his eyes searching hers. "Dance with me."

CHAPTER 26

Safe in River's arms, Hazel soon forgot there were other couples dancing around them. She closed her eyes and swayed to the music enveloping them like the warm, moonlit waters of some mystical southern sea. River's embrace was tender but firm, as if she were precious and delicate and he had no intention of letting her go again.

When the song changed into a slower, sweeter tune, River's breath brushed over her cheek. "Hey, beautiful."

Hazel opened her eyes. The soft light of lanterns and fairy lights played on River's face, illuminating the plane of his forehead, the line of his brow, the angle of his jaw.

Hazel smiled. "Hey, handsome."

His arms tightened a little more, pulling her closer and enveloping her with his heady scent. "It's a problem, the way I see so little of you when I'm working all day," he murmured, his lips moving against her hair.

Hazel let her head come to rest on his shoulder. As if the new melody was a charm to unlock her heart, images suddenly poured from it. Not the images of a dream, shapeless and vague and easily forgotten. But real images, so crisp and clear that every facet and every nuance was lit. Of a future together, of happiness as deep as the sea, of a soft, silky love rarely granted to penniless, unimportant dressmakers on small islands.

But maybe River didn't think she was unimportant.

And maybe a small island could be all the world if the right person lived on it.

The sweet, slow tune came to an end, morphing into a faster rhythm. Hazel lifted her head to look at River. No longer did a smile play on his lips or in his eyes. In the flickering light, his blue irises looked like a stormy sea ready to swallow her, and the heat coming from his lips felt like a fire on a cold night.

A small gasp escaped Hazel's throat as she took in the change in his features.

He pulled her to him, closing the last gap between them. "You," he murmured, letting her hand go and taking her in his arms.

"And you," she breathed, wrapping her own arms around his neck.

"I've never felt like this before," he murmured. "Tell me you feel it too."

Hazel's eyelids fluttered. "I feel it too." It wasn't electricity that made her—all of her, heart, mind, and body—vibrate. It wasn't something as fleeting or easily turned off. It was intense and strong and demanding, coursing between them like a stream rushing down a cliff to meet the sea. Overwhelmed, she lowered her gaze.

"Look at me. Let me see you." River loosened his hold to put a finger under her chin and tilt her face to his.

There was no longer any mistaking the light in his stormy eyes or the way he held her. There was no more doubt in Hazel's mind, and no other question to ask. Suddenly, it was the most natural thing in the world for her to touch him, and she traced her fingers down the line of his temple and jaw, feeling the cleanly shaved skin, the hollow of his cheek, the dip in the center of his chin that now was hers.

River caught her fingers in his hand, pressing a kiss to each one before placing her hand on his chest. Then he slowed their dance to a halt and lowered his lips to hers.

The taste of red wine and caramel filled her senses as they shared a long, delicious, soul-spinning kiss. A kiss, not a peck on the cheek or a blessing on the forehead. A kiss like a current joining the sea, a kiss as hot as the sun and as deep as the universe.

River broke away first.

"Come." He took her hand in his, and without hesitation, Hazel followed him. They went down a short flight of fieldstone stairs and walked through starlit rows of grapevines until the twinkle lights and the sound of the music faded behind them. When they found a soft spot of grass and fallen leaves with a view of the vineyard hills, their slopes veiled by the night, they stopped.

River sat down and pulled Hazel onto his lap. "Are you warm enough?" he murmured, kissing her neck.

The air was mild, but the way his lips pressed against her sensitive skin made Hazel shiver. She leaned into him. "I am when you hold me," she whispered.

He hugged her closer, caressing her bare arms, igniting her with his touch. Hazel exhaled a shaky breath, full of longing and desire.

"I know," he murmured. "I feel the same. Let's sit for a moment."

Hazel let her head sink against this chest, and for a long while, the two of them watched more and more stars appear in the velvety blue sky until the firmament was sprinkled with gold and silver. A breeze rustled the grape leaves above them. Now and then, the muffled sound of music and dancing drifted past them like the laughter of night sprites.

"Are you sure about you and me?" she finally whispered. "It's going to be different. Do you want that?"

"From the moment I saw you," he murmured and turned just enough to see her face. "I really thought I was going mad because I've never felt like this. It was too much, too soon."

She smiled. "*Are* you going mad?"

He smiled back. "Would it bother you?"

She shook her head. "What about...the things you said before? About being on the rebound?"

He shook his head once, as if he were unwilling to hear the words repeated. "I've never felt about my ex the way I feel about you." His muscles tightened. "I tiptoed on eggshells around her, thinking that for some reason, I had to make it work."

"Why?"

He shrugged. "Maybe losing my dad made me hold on to her, thinking it was one relationship I could save. I don't know. Now I'm glad it's over. She's gone from my life and my thoughts."

"Will I be gone from your thoughts too if you leave the cove again?"

"No. You touch my heart." He trailed a finger along her collarbone. "It hurts my soul how beautiful you are. We can grow as old as stone together, and you'll still take my breath away."

Hazel felt her own heart and soul open; no longer could she protect herself. She wanted River; if he left her again, so be it. Until he did, she wanted to kiss him, love him, hold his hand, and dance in his arms.

Their lips met in a passionate, urgent kiss. For the first time, Hazel allowed herself to feel the full intensity of her love for River. She broke away, her heart drumming in her veins. "This scares me! I think I'm mad too. I've never...*never*..."

"I know." He took a breath. "Let's not be scared of each other. We aren't mad for being in love. Let's not think it can't work because it's too good. Let's give us a chance. I want that. I want it more than anything."

"You are in love?" she whispered. "Really?"

"I think I am." He shook his head and blew out a breath, impatient with himself. "No. I don't *think*. I know. I know I'm in love. I want you. All of you. This..."

He let his fingers run through her hair, to the nape of her neck. His touch sent shivers of anticipation down her bare shoulders. "This." He leaned in and took his time kissing her mouth. "And *this*." He kissed her on the forehead. "I want it all."

Hazel reached up and pulled his lips back to hers, wrapping her arms around him and letting River know that she, too, wanted all of him. Body, heart, and soul. He was hers, and she was his.

"Are *you* sure you want this?" He smiled against her lips as he lowered her into the sweet-smelling leaves that softly blanketed the ground in a red carpet that glowed in the moonlight.

Instead of replying, Hazel closed her eyes. And when River kissed the spot between her collarbones, Hazel arched her back, giving him all the answers he needed.

CHAPTER 27

Jon put his arm around Jenny and kissed the top of her head. Jenny was just about to kiss him back when she spotted the car entering their brand-new, cobbled driveway.

"There they are!" She let go of Jon and waved. From the open windows, several hands appeared and waved back.

Jenny wanted to jump with excitement. She'd ordered the kids to stay away during the roof construction of her and Jon's new house in the vineyard so she could show off her new house in all its finished glory. Finally, the moment had come.

River parked his car, and he, Audrey, and Hazel jumped out.

"Mom! It's *beautiful*!" Audrey ran to her and slung her arms around Jenny.

"Hi, sweetheart! You like it?" Laughing, Jenny caught her daughter while River offered Jon his hand.

Grinning, Jon grabbed it only to pull River into a bear hug. "Good to see you, River."

"You too, Jon." He grinned.

Jenny couldn't remember when she'd last seen River this happy and relaxed, and he wasn't even on vacation. Clearly, dating Hazel did him a world of good.

"I'm glad you were able to make time, River," she said. "We know you're busy." She smiled.

"Wouldn't have missed the big reveal for the world, Mom." River looked over his shoulder, and Jenny followed her son's gaze.

Hazel still stood by the car, her pretty, polka-dotted vintage dress fluttering in the wind as she waited for the family to greet each other.

Of course Audrey had told Jenny the old story that intertwined their family with Hazel's. But none of it was the young dressmaker's fault. "Go on in, darling," Jenny whispered to Audrey. "Have a look at the kitchen; the new stove has arrived. Jon was going to hook it up last night, but the full moon was just too lovely. We watched it from the hot tub and forgot the time."

"I can't believe you have a hot tub. By the way, I'm keeping a swimsuit in this house."

"You do that, darling." Jenny kissed her daughter's cheek.

"Let's go! I'll show you how the hot tub controls work, so you can use it anytime you feel like it," Jon said and gestured toward the door.

Excited to see the new additions to the house, Audrey grabbed River's arm.

"Go ahead. I want to show Hazel the new flower bed." Smiling, Jenny went to meet Hazel.

The young woman stiffened ever so slightly when she saw Jenny coming toward her.

Their first meeting, like the pasts of their families, had set them off on the wrong foot. It was time to straighten things out.

"Hazel," Jenny said warmly. "How are you?"

"Good. Thank you." Hazel nodded. "I'm... I hope it's okay I tagged along. River asked me to come."

"I'm glad he did."

"It's so beautiful here. I didn't know."

Jenny smiled. "Isn't it? I love it too."

The spot Jon had chosen was conveniently close to the winery and offered the most enchanting view on the entire estate. The front of the house hugged the vineyard, while the backyard blended into a forest of widely spaced, mature oaks. A charming path led through them to the bubbling creek that was the lifeline of the vineyard.

"Listen, darling." Jenny took Hazel's arm and led her to the wide flower bed that wrapped, still waiting to be planted, around the house's foundation. "I want us to put the past behind us once and for all."

Hazel glanced at her. "You do?"

"Jon and I just built a house. I loved every minute of it, but it was a whole thing on top of teaching and running the winery. I promise the last thing I'm interested in is holding a grudge over a dress."

The set of Hazel's shoulders dropped. "I'm so sorry about dangling it in front of you," she said, the words tumbling out quickly. "I hope you know that personally, I would *love* for you to wear the dress at your wedding."

Jenny nodded. "But you made your family a promise, and I like that you stand up for it." She smiled. "Trust me when I say that I love integrity more than satin and lace."

"Okay." Finally, the corners of Hazel's lips lifted. "Thank you."

"Audrey told me about Marianne and Robert," Jenny said.

Hazel blinked, her eyes worried. "I had no idea about what happened. I only found out together with Audrey."

"I know. I also have no intention of nursing a grudge over anything that might have happened to Marianne. It had nothing to do with you, after all." Jenny paused to take a breath. Marianne was family. Sometime, somehow, Jenny would have to find out more about her. "Let's make a new beginning together."

A sweet smile spread from Hazel's mouth to her eyes. "I'd like that," she said. "But Robert was a relative of mine. If he did something to Marianne... It makes me feel terrible. I'm going to keep digging. I'll search until I find out what happened and where Marianne is."

Jenny took Hazel's hands into her own. "Don't feel terrible any longer, please."

River stepped out of the front door just then, and Hazel's eyes flickered to him.

Jenny smiled. "Let's have a tour of the house." Impulsively, she hugged Hazel. "Come on. It's too pretty a corner of the world to hold on to anything but love and friendship."

"It is." Hazel smiled at Jenny, and then she went to where River was waiting for them. He took Hazel's hand, and they went inside, passing Jon.

He came to Jenny. "I'd say those two are in it for the long term, don't you think? They look good together." Jon put his arm around her waist.

"I agree." Jenny leaned into Jon.

"Who knows, maybe they're the ones who will finally marry." Jon chuckled, and they started walking toward the house. "A second chance to join the families." He opened the door for her.

"We'll see." She stepped inside, smiling, and then she called out for the kids to join them so they could start a proper tour.

Their little group wandered through the house, the kids oohing and aahing and admiring all the details.

Their house in the vineyard was smaller than the majestic old mansion at Beach and Forgotten, and smaller even than the ever-expanding winery on the hill. But it was ample space for Jenny and Jon, and there were four bedrooms upstairs for friends and kids to stay over. Maybe, Jenny thought as she watched River and Hazel walk arm in arm, even grandkids.

Jon had built the house in the style of the winery, and everywhere was glass, rich wood, natural light, and greenery. They had added just enough modern touches to make everything as comfortable as it could be.

The kitchen was Jon's favorite. They had splurged on high-end appliances and plenty of counter space so he could cook to his heart's content. Jenny's favorite room in the house was her spacious, modern bathroom. It had a ceiling-to-floor window and a sunken tub, which made her feel like she was bathing in a forest pool.

Their favorite piece of furniture, they agreed, was the long, wide table a carpenter friend had made from a slab of redwood from the Donovan sawmill. The rich wood gleamed warmly in the rays of the October sun falling through the floor-to-ceiling windows as they passed it, and Jenny gave it a fond pat. It was perfect for hosting their large combined family.

Slowly, their group broke up as everyone spread out.

"Hey, did you go out on the wrap-around balcony yet?" Audrey called out to River, who was in Jenny's bright new office, admiring an orchid. She had always loved their graceful flowers, and Jon had surprised her with several large, blooming Phalaenopsis and Cymbidiums in simple, hand-thrown pots.

"No!" River set the orchid back on the bookshelf. "Be there in a minute!"

Jenny sat in her chair behind the wide glass desk and smiled at her eldest. "You look happy," she said.

"So do you. I'm glad you decided to move back to Mendocino Cove, Mom. I'm glad everything worked out the way it did."

Jenny leaned forward. "I like Hazel." She hesitated. "Are you sure it's not too early for another relationship? I'd hate to see you hurt again. Or her, to be honest."

River crossed his hands behind him. "For a while, I thought it *was* too early. That I had to wait some nebulous amount of time to heal more." He shook his head. "When I arrived in the cove, I was determined not to date for at least a year. But with Hazel..." Suddenly, he closed his eyes. When he opened them again, he smiled. "I'm just glad I didn't get engaged before, Mom. You have no idea."

Relaxing, Jenny smiled back at her wonderful son. "Well then, darling, if that's how you feel...take good care of her. And this time, make sure to take good care of yourself too."

CHAPTER 28

Patiently, Hazel waited until the curtain to the changing room finally opened. Jenny came out first, lifting the curtain wide for Faye.

Faye stepped into the bright sunlight flooding the little store. The wedding gown swirled around her, and the smile on her face told Hazel everything she had wanted to know.

"What magic is this?" Faye let go of the helping hand and turned. The skirt flared like a blossoming flower. "How can a bit of fabric make me feel like a queen?"

"It's a *lot* of fabric," Jenny said. "Careful with the twirling. Don't step on it and stumble again. Hazel can probably do with a little less drama than last time."

Hazel smiled, delighted with the way the fabric moved. She tugged on it, checking the length. "You look very beautiful, Faye. Should we take the hem in just a little higher in the front?"

"I think so." Faye studied her reflection in the tall mirror. "I really don't want to stumble when I walk down the aisle." She put her hands on her belly, clearly remembering the last tumble she took.

"It won't take long." Hazel kneeled and, with Jenny's help, pinned the hem. The wedding was close, and this was the last alteration Faye needed for the dress to fit perfectly. When it was done, she stood, pushing the leftover needles back into her strawberry-shaped pincushion. "The bust and waist are perfect." She scrutinized the rest of the dress. "I think it's great. How do you feel?"

"Perfect. It did feel just a bit loose before," Faye said and tilted her head as she studied her reflection. "I've grown into it just so."

Satisfied, Hazel put down the pincushion and picked up her phone. "Can you stand straight and look at me? I want to take a photo for reference when sewing the hem. Your wedding is in a week, and the dress needs to be ready when you are."

"Sure." Faye squared her shoulders and smiled.

"Are you nervous at all, Faye?" Jenny asked while Hazel took her photos.

"I should be, shouldn't I?" Faye lifted her arms when Hazel asked her to. "But I'm not. I can't *wait*. I can't wait to marry Gabe, and I also can't wait to have this baby. Maybe the nerves will come later?"

"Maybe. I remember being so nervous I was shaking." Jenny held a pearl comb with an attached veil to Faye's hair. "How's that?"

Faye waved the veil away. "No, don't be silly. I don't want a veil. I'm not a blushing bride and big as I am, I'm already scared of stumbling. If I wear heels, I at least want to see the ground with laser-like precision."

Laughing, Jenny returned the veil to the display. "What are you going to do with your hair? You can't wear a messy bun in case that was your plan."

Faye narrowed her eyes at her friend. "Hazel? The bun looks good, doesn't it?"

"Of course it does." Hazel cleared her throat delicately. "But I would suggest balancing the baby bump with open, flowing hair. You could emphasize your natural curls with pearl or flower pins."

"Oooh, that sounds nice. How do I do it?"

"I used to have a friend on Lover's Lane who did gorgeous bridal hairdos." Hazel went to get a pack of pearl pins. "She moved to Los Angeles a year ago, but she taught me a thing or two before she left. May I?"

"Yep." Faye unceremoniously pulled out the scrunchie that held her curls on top of her head. Her light-brown waves fell past her shoulders, thick and shining. "It's growing like crazy, and I haven't cut it in a while." She raked her fingers through it. "Do you need a brush? I have one." She fished one from her purse and handed it over.

Hazel swept the hair loosely out of Faye's face, braided a few small sections and twisted others, then pinned the strands in an intricate pattern and fastened everything with a scatter of shimmering pearl pins.

"There. What do you think?" Hazel stepped back, satisfied. The warm light gleamed on the luscious, soft hair, and the pearls provided that touch of bridal magic that had been missing before.

Faye turned to the mirror. "Oh!" Her eyes widened. "That's really beautiful. Huh!" She touched her hair as if she couldn't quite believe it was her own.

"Gabe's going to cry when he sees you," Jenny predicted happily.

Faye sighed dreamily. "Can I wear my hair like this every day?" She turned her head this way and that, trying to see the back.

"Bridal pearls in the supermarket? No. Wait for me before you change. I'll need a moment to powder my nose." Jenny nodded in the direction of the bathroom and left.

Hazel adjusted another mirror so Faye could inspect the back. "Do you like the beading right here? Do you want more? Less?"

Faye studied her back, and for a while, they discussed the pros and cons of minor adjustments until Faye finally decided the dress was perfect as it was. "I'd better get out of this," she said. "I'm starting to like it too much, and in a moment, I'm just going to walk out the door like this. Why shouldn't we wear wedding dresses all the time? Who says it has to always be jeans and flannel shirts in the supermarket? Let me be a beautiful queen in satin when I want to!"

"Uh-oh, the urge is taking over." Hazel laughed. "Let's get out of it so I can fix the hem. What you do with the dress after that is up to you. And if you want to wear it to the supermarket, I'll support that."

"I mean, I wish I had the guts to do it. But I don't want to be the only one." Hazel sighed, clearly resigning herself to reality. "All right. Fine."

Smiling, Hazel turned to see if the rustling behind her meant that Jenny was coming back to help their pregnant bride with her change.

Instead, she spotted Jenny standing by a dress rack. In her hand was the sleeve of her own special dress, and she was studying it wistfully, her thumb caressing the fabric. When she noted Hazel's gaze, she quickly dropped it.

"Busted," Jenny said, with an embarrassed laugh.

"Jenny..." Hazel exhaled softly.

"No, it's nothing. Never mind, Hazel. I just wanted to see—" She shrugged and turned away from the rack, pushing her hands into the pockets of her jeans. "I just wanted to see if you still had it."

Hazel flushed warmly. She knew Jenny better now. She certainly knew her well enough to know that her laugh missed its ring.

Jenny joined Hazel and Faye in front of the mirror. "Seriously, never mind, Hazel," she said lightly. "I was just curious."

"I didn't sell it," Hazel murmured.

Faye sighed and affectionately bumped Jenny with her shoulder. "Didn't your new dress come in the mail yesterday?"

"Yes!" Jenny said, too quickly, too brightly. "Yes, it did."

"And?" Hazel asked without much hope. "Did you try it on?"

"Yes." Jenny smiled bravely. "I did, and it's fabulous. I might order another one too, since there's still time. Faye, come on, let's get your queenly behind back in your maternity pants. Jon and Gabe are probably already waiting for us at the ferry. Hazel, do you have all the measurements and photos you need?"

Hazel nodded and held open the curtain to the changing room for Faye and Jenny, who disappeared into it. Then, quietly, Hazel went to the clothes rack. Jenny's dress was still pulled halfway out, the delicate fabric shining softly in the sunlight.

She lifted the hanger of the rod and draped the dress over her arm.

After all, Hazel was a dressmaker deep down. It was her calling to make women feel beautiful, and Jenny had become a friend. If she couldn't have the dress so clearly meant for her, Hazel wasn't going to sell it to anyone else either. At least not until long after Jenny's wedding was over.

Hazel brought the dress into the atelier and hung it up on a rack of works in progress. Then she hurried back, arriving just as the two friends re-emerged.

Hazel took Faye's gown, careful of the pinned hem. "I'll call you when it's done," she promised. "It won't take long."

They exchanged hugs and thanks, and then Hazel's friends left. She waited until the bell had stopped ringing before she brought this dress into the back too. On her way back, she stopped at the door and, giving in to an impulse, turned to look at her small atelier.

A long time ago, Klara had leaned over this table to design the pattern for her first wedding gown.

Her design sketch still hung on the wall, the frame tarnished with age. Slowly, Hazel reached up, letting her finger run over the blind, corded silver.

Through generations, the women in the family faithfully adhered to the patterns Klara had crafted. Each taught their knowledge to the next, forging a chain that bound mothers and daughters together as tightly as quality thread unites bodice and skirt.

Hazel curled her fingers around the old-fashioned frame.

Times changed. Hearts changed, and so did souls.

She lifted the heavy frame off the nail. Dust motes that had clung to the brown-paper backing whirled into the air like soiled snow.

Hazel carried the frame to the window and pushed the glass panes open. With a deep breath, she blew the dust outside, watching as the breeze joyfully whisked it out to the sea.

Leaving the window ajar to air the atelier, Hazel laid the pattern upside down on her worktable. With a metal ruler, she started to pry off the tiny nails that held the frame together.

Sometimes, generational patterns had to change. Sometimes, daughters understood more than their mothers. And sometimes, promises should be broken.

Love and friendship had opened Hazel's eyes.

It was time for a fresh start.

CHAPTER 29

"Ready?" Audrey smiled at Hazel, glad for the chance to spend time with River's girlfriend. Usually, Hazel was busy making the rounds with River or designing new dresses.

"I'm ready. Let's do this." Hazel pretended to roll up her sleeves when in fact, she wore a cute sleeveless blouse that complemented her navy capri pants.

"There's much to do," Audrey admitted as she led the way to the stairs. "The attic is huge and crammed full of things."

"Bring it on." Hazel looked undaunted. "I'm dying to dig for treasure in your attic. It can't all be boring clutter."

"Oh." Audrey started climbing. "I already know there's treasure; I just haven't made much progress discovering it. My goal so far has been to shove things into neat piles to pass inspection. But once that's done, I'm absolutely spending all my evenings up there, digging through every sealed hat box and forgotten hope chest."

"*All* your evenings? Really?"

Audrey grinned down at Hazel. "Hey—not all of us have someone warm to cuddle at night. If I had a man as besotted with me as River is with you, I'd probably spend my evenings kissing instead of exploring old attics too. But there's nobody in sight. I'll have to make do. Beggars can't be choosers, you know."

"Audrey, that's not what I meant at all." Even in the dim light of the staircase, the glow spreading over Hazel's fair skin was visible. "You make it sound like I was rubbing it in."

Laughing, Audrey pulled herself through the attic opening, then helped her friend. "Never mind, I'm just teasing you." She brushed dust off Hazel's shoulder. "I'm really glad you and River found each other."

"You'll find someone too," Hazel murmured, rubbing her cheek as if she could erase the color.

"Yeah, right." Audrey sighed. "Tall, handsome, dark, eager to hold my hand... I can see him now."

"Mysterious," Hazel helped her out and grinned. "With a dash of enigma."

"Rich."

"*Super* rich. *At least* a billionaire."

They both laughed, and Audrey waved Hazel to follow her. "Look. This is the suitcase that belonged to Marianne. Or at least, it's the suitcase with the diary in the lining." She kneeled on the wooden floor and lifted the heavy lid.

"What else is in it?" Hazel also kneeled beside the case, peering at the contents. "What's all this?"

"I don't know, just clothes. There's nothing else tucked into the lining. I checked."

"They are never *just* clothes," Hazel murmured. "Clothes can tell you a lot about a person."

"Says the dressmaker." The light filtering through the old windows was soft and scattered, and Audrey squinted, wishing she'd remembered to buy a strong, bright flashlight. She leaned closer. "What's that? A skirt?"

Hazel smiled and unfolded the fabric. "Audrey, how can it be a skirt? It's a towel."

"Aha. Good, I'm glad they saved all their old towels. I can't wait to toss them on their behalf." Again, Audrey was only teasing Hazel—the towel was old, the once-white cotton yellowed with age, but clearly it was unused. Someone had taken the time to stitch a flouncy letter into the corner.

"Noo," Hazel protested, inspecting the stitching. "Do not toss this. It's precious. Someone hemmed this by hand. I'm sure the local museum would be happy to have a few pieces if you don't want them."

Audrey lifted the monogrammed corner. "Look. It's a letter." She tilted her head. "Hazel, it's an M. M for Marianne."

"She stopped stitching before she was quite finished. Her last name is still missing, but she started it here." Hazel ran a finger over the raised thread before putting the towel back. "Then this *is* her suitcase. This was probably part of her wedding trousseau."

Audrey unfolded another piece, the fabric stiff from the passage of time. "What's this, another towel?"

Hazel glanced over. "It's a pillowcase."

"To think she had to make all these bed linens, knowing what sort of marriage waited for her with Robert... That can't have been easy." Audrey set the pillowcase back.

Hazel nodded. "I wonder why she hid the diary. It would have been safer to get rid of it."

"The story you record in a diary is part of you. You don't just throw that away." Audrey chuckled. "Actually, I tried to do that once, after a bad breakup. But it was so wrong that I went outside in the middle of the night to fish it out of the trash can again. Now it lives in my secret drawer. I sincerely hope nobody will ever find it."

"Burning is the only correct way of getting rid of diaries, anyway. Never toss them in a can. Hey. What's this?" Hazel pointed at a piece of paper wedged between the wall of the suitcase and a stack of linen.

Audrey's eyebrows rose. "Maybe it slipped from the top of the stack when I moved the suitcase last time. Hang on." Gently, Audrey wiggled the paper out.

"Is it a letter?" Hazel squinted.

"It's not folded. It's nothing. Just a piece of paper." Disappointed, Audrey dropped it back.

Hazel picked it up and frowned. "Audrey, I swear there's something written on it. Use your phone flashlight."

Audrey pulled out her phone and tapped the screen, then held the light over the paper. "You're right. Really faint, in pencil. It's a name? I think it's a name."

"What name? Marianne?"

"Her—" Audrey changed the angle of the light to see the faded marks. "Herbert Whit—man."

"Herbert Whitman? What has he got to do with anything?" Hazel murmured. "Why would Marianne have a piece of paper with the name *Herbert* written on it in her trousseau?"

"The handwriting is nothing like in her diary," Audrey said. "If it weren't so faint, I could easily read it. Either Marianne was concealing her handwriting in the diary, or someone else wrote this."

"Who else would have done that? Not Robert. He doesn't strike me as the type to put other men's names in with his wife's trousseau."

Audrey switched off the flashlight. "Marianne disappeared before they got married. Robert wouldn't have had access to her suitcases in the first place."

"That's right." Hazel looked up. "I'm sorry, I shouldn't have said that. I feel terrible about what Robert did to Marianne."

"We don't know what he did," Audrey reminded her friend softly. "Not for sure. But he wouldn't have put the note in here."

"Then it was Marianne?"

"I don't know that she could've concealed her handwriting this much. Maybe it was one of her relatives."

"Her mother?"

Audrey nodded. "Or her grandmother, Phoebe. Did you know that as a young girl, Phoebe and her sweetheart stole a whaler in Nantucket and sailed off into the sunset? That's how our family came to the cove."

"Goodness."

"Phoebe doesn't strike me as a woman who would let her granddaughter marry an abuser."

"But Marianne wrote in her diary that she couldn't confide in anyone. Maybe Phoebe didn't realize what was happening."

Audrey doubted that very much. According to the diary, Robert had put down Marianne more than once in front of her family. "Sooner or later, they'd have caught on. His behavior escalated with every entry Marianne made. Her family *must* have noticed it." Audrey took a deep breath. She'd been thinking it over for a while. "Any grandmother worth her salt would go in, saber swinging, to get Marianne out of an engagement like that. And Phoebe was an old pirate who believed in true love. She would have made sure Marianne was safe."

"You think Phoebe helped Marianne to get away from Robert?" Hazel's voice lifted with hope. "That would be great, wouldn't it?"

"Yeah. It would be." Audrey took a photo of the slip of paper before gently setting it back. "Whoever brought the suitcase up here could tell us more about Marianne."

"Maybe they were also the ones who wrote the name on the paper and put it in there."

"Let's find out who this Herbert is." Audrey closed the suitcase and stood, brushing the dust off her knees.

Hazel followed her example. She hugged herself, rubbing her bare arms. "Aren't we supposed to clean up for the fire inspector?"

Audrey looked around. "Sometimes, a girl's gotta do some sleuthing first. Besides, it's good enough."

"Really?" Hazel looked doubtful into the dark vastness of the attic. "What's back there?"

"I haven't been." Audrey grinned. "I still have time before the inspection. I'll pull a couple of all-nighters if I have to."

"Then...how do we sleuth?" Hazel spread her hands. "We can't randomly search for a clue in all the boxes and cases and chests up here. There's just too many hiding spots."

"Oh, we can do better than random searches. We don't live in the Dark Ages." Audrey raised an arm, pointing at the light falling through the ceiling. "To the library!"

CHAPTER 30

I t's perfect." Hazel arranged the dress so that the skirt flared out behind Faye. It fit just so, and the soft material shimmered, beautiful and precious, in the sunlight of a Mendocino wedding day.

Nervously, Faye touched her intricate braids of hair. "This pin here is poking me, Hazel. Can you fix it?"

Jenny, dressed in a long lilac silk dress, joined them behind the thick wax myrtle bushes. Their wind-tousled branches gracefully swayed in the coastal breeze, hiding the bridal party from the wedding guests and groom on the bluff. "Faye, I think Gabe's going to faint if you don't get out there right now. I'm not joking. Jon is getting ready to catch him."

Quickly, Hazel pulled out the offensive pin. "Is this better?" One pearl more or less hardly mattered when the groom's knees were about to buckle.

"Better." Faye squared her shoulders and held out a hand. "Flowers," she whispered.

Billie lifted her own lilac dress and pressed the slim bouquet of calla lilies in the bride's hand. "There you go, pumpkin. Good luck."

"Ready?" Faye looked at Billie, who looked at Jenny, who looked at Ava, who nodded.

"Ladies, let's do this," Billie ordered, and the three friends lined up in front of Faye. "Okay. We'll walk up the path. Gabe and the minister stand to the right. Faye goes left, we mirror the groomsmen. Standard issue. Any last questions or concerns?"

"I'm dizzy," Faye said weakly.

"No!" Billie lifted a warning finger. "Gabe is already feeling faint. Pull yourself together, sister."

"Okay." Faye took a deep breath. Her skin was almost as pale as her dress. "Ready."

"Music," Billie said nervously.

Smiling, Hazel gave her an encouraging thumbs-up and then hurried down a narrow path that led to the bride's side of the bluff.

"Music," Hazel mouthed at Lex, Billie's cousin, who was already waiting, phone in hand, to play the wedding march from the speakers hidden high up in a cypress. Lex pressed his button, wiggled a wire, and the sound of music rose into the air like a larch.

The familiar tune quickly quieted the waiting guests, and an expectant silence gave way to the charming melody. Hazel slipped into her chair and took a deep breath. Her part in the preparations was over. Now, she could enjoy the ceremony that was about to unfold like the wings of a butterfly, just the same as all the others and yet uniquely beautiful.

"All right?" Smiling, River took her hand in his.

"All right," she whispered. "Faye looks gorgeous. It was touch and go with the hair and the wind, but she didn't notice. It's good now."

"You did great." He squeezed her hand. "How are they doing back there?"

"Good." She smiled back. "Bit nervous. Ready to get married."

"I bet." There was no teasing light in his eyes, and he didn't smile as he held her gaze.

The familiar warmth crept up Hazel's throat, and she swiped a hand over her glowing cheek to break away from his spell. Surely it was only in her mind that River was searching her face for an answer to an unasked question. They'd only been dating for such a short time...

Confused, Hazel opened her clutch and rummaged around for her fan. It was a warm day, and the bright sun filtered through the feathery boughs of cedars and cypresses. She started fanning herself to cool down, giving River an apologetic look when he turned to see what she was doing now.

He pressed his lips together as if he was trying not to smile.

Raising an eyebrow, Hazel nodded for him to stop looking at her and pay attention to the sandy path that doubled as the bride's aisle.

Gabe, the groom, had his hands folded in front of him and was staring up at the cedar branches that formed a natural arch above and framed the glistening ocean below.

To Hazel, he didn't look like he was about to faint. Instead, Gabe had the air of a man weighing his duty to wait with the desire to storm into the bushes and check on his woman.

Hazel smiled. Marriage could be hard. But nothing would come between these two. She had been to enough weddings to know which couples would stick it out.

"Here they come," River whispered and craned his neck. "There's Billie. And Mom. They look so good."

Hazel put a hand on his arm to let him know she'd heard but kept her own eyes on the groom. This was the moment brides dreamed about when they came into her store on Lover's Lane. This was the moment Hazel would never tire of watching.

Gabe's hands opened, his eyes widened, and a huge breath strained his tuxedo.

Behind him, his best man, Jon, mouthed a silent *whoa*.

That was the effect a dressmaker was looking for. Smiling, Hazel turned to watch the bridal party.

Billie emerged first from the wax myrtles. She carried a single calla lily in her hand and walked determinedly toward the minister. Behind her came Jenny, always graceful, then Ava, smiling brightly. Next, Faye herself appeared.

"She looks wonderful." Hazel felt a tear spill from her eye as she watched. "I've sat through a hundred weddings, but it gets me every time."

"Don't be sorry. I think it's sweet." Smiling, River pulled a tissue from the pocket of his tuxedo and handed it to her.

Audrey leaned around her brother to catch Hazel's eye. "You okay?" she mouthed. She herself was dry-eyed and beaming, and clearly enjoying the occasion.

"Yeah, thanks," Hazel whispered. She smiled sheepishly at her friend, dabbing her eyes.

The bride reached the groom, and it was clear that he thought she was the most beautiful woman in the world. Hazel let herself sink into the ceremony. The dress was perfection itself; the high empire waist allowed the skirt to flow freely, and the different layers moved gently in the light wind, complementing Faye's figure instead of hiding it and giving the bride an ethereal look.

"Hazel?" River touched her arm when people started applauding. "They've kissed. It's over."

Hazel rose with the others to cheer the freshly married couple. Waving and laughing, radiant with happiness, Faye and Gabe passed through their cheering guests who tossed flower petals and rice. A car was already waiting to whisk them to the reception at the winery.

Everyone filed out of the narrow rows of folding chairs, laughing and talking about the event. River took Hazel's hand. Together with many other guests, they walked along the bluff to the small, sandy lot where they had parked.

Audrey, who had been walking ahead of them, fell back. "Hazel, the dress was just gorgeous."

"It did look good, didn't it?"

Audrey nodded. "You need to *please* do something about that dress Mom bought, though."

"Audrey," River grumbled.

His sister sighed. "Yeah, I know. But, Riv, you haven't seen it. It's nothing like the sales picture online. Hazel, I hate to ask. But could you at least make the dress fit Mom?"

"Of course." Hazel smiled at Audrey. "I was already going to ask if I could take a look."

"Yes, please do. It just hangs on her, and she can't be bothered to find another one. She's tired of looking at gowns, let alone trying them on, and she's starting to say that this one is fine."

It was like that once a woman found her dress. After wearing *the one*, the fun of trying on more wedding dresses was gone. There really was no going back.

"I'll do what I can," Hazel promised.

"Thanks," Audrey said, relief in her voice, and merged back into the crowd.

"You don't have to do anything, you know." River put an arm around Hazel. "I know the whole dress thing still gets to you. I want you to be happy. We all do."

Safe, loved, and very much in love herself, Hazel smiled at her handsome young doctor. "Hearing you say that means the world to me, River. But I already asked your mom if I could talk to her about the wedding dress."

CHAPTER 31

Jenny dabbed her eyes, waving at the newlyweds' car as it wound its way down the vineyard hill. "There they go." She shivered in the fresh morning air, rubbing her arms for warmth.

Most guests who had come to see off the married couple watched until the car disappeared from view. Laughing, chatting, and recalling memories of their own honeymoons, they soon after turned to go back inside. Everyone had had champagne and mimosas to cheer the married couple, and now, Jon and Hannah were waiting with a luxurious breakfast buffet. Even outside in the winery's parking lot, the cool air was full of the tantalizing, beckoning scents of freshly brewed coffee, warm buttery croissants, crisp bacon, and sweet waffles with maple syrup.

Audrey joined Jenny, pulling her merino shawl tight around her shoulders. "How long will they be gone?"

"A week in Hawaii and a week here at home to get the nursery ready." Jenny slipped her arm under her daughter's. "They'll be so happy."

"Happy and busy." Audrey shaded her eyes against the bright, cool morning sun. "I hear a new baby is a lot of work."

Jenny smiled. "Faye has me, Ava, and Billie. We still remember the tricks of the trade. But you're right. It's a grueling slog."

"I'm sorry you had to go through that." Audrey shook her head. "Also, you're *welcome* because I'm a *great* daughter."

"Worth every stinky diaper, for sure." Jenny grabbed Audrey and smacked a kiss on each of her cheeks.

Laughing, Audrey wiggled free to catch her slipping shawl. "Let's go inside, Mom. The cold is getting to you."

They joined the other guests inside the winery. "You and Jon are next, Mom." Audrey poured herself a hot chocolate, warming her hands on the mug before taking a sip of the creamy liquid. She sighed happily. "Mh-mm. This hits the spot after the cold. You know, I really love Mendocino weddings." Appreciatively, she lifted her drink. "Make sure you throw a brunch party the day after your wedding, please. I need more buffets in my life."

"It's only going to be a quick ceremony and a dinner with family and close friends, darling." Jenny smiled at her daughter. "If you want a big wedding, marry yourself. Jon will throw you the best breakfast buffet you've ever seen. Flowers, chocolate fountain, balloon arches...whatever you want."

Audrey laughed at the idea of marrying herself. "Nah. Better you than me, if you know what I mean. I'm too young, and I don't have time for all that jazz. Not to mention that I don't even have a man in my life."

"You'll make time when he finds you, darling." Jenny tilted her head. She would have liked to say a lot more about the subject to her daughter. Like how she was sorry that most young people left Mendocino Cove to find work. How Audrey should probably go out sometimes to meet someone. How it would be good if Billie's boys could visit more often.

Then again, Audrey was still young, and she was smart. She didn't need to be told the obvious.

Instead of talking, Jenny gave herself a silent promise to act. One way or the other, she would get more young people to visit the cove. After all, she was a college professor, and many of her students were tired of living in the on-campus dorms. Even new faculty moving into the area often had a hard time finding affordable housing.

Once the hotel opened, they could offer a special semester rate for students and faculty...

Instinctively, her eyes searched for her best friend and soulmate. She soon spotted Jon standing behind the buffet table, stacking a freshly baked batch of steaming mini quiches onto serving stands.

As if feeling her gaze on him, Jon looked up. When their eyes met, he put a hand to his heart and blew a kiss. Smiling back, Jenny shook her head at him.

Audrey nudged Jenny's arm. "Mom, I'm going to take Aunt Georgie back to the hotel before she finishes all the mimosas in front of her, all right? The builders are coming to put in the ramp in an hour. I'll see you tomorrow."

"See you tomorrow, sweetheart." Jenny made her way to her own table and collected her clutch, waving at friends and neighbors clamoring for her to sit.

"Jenny?" Hazel came to meet her. She'd sat with Audrey since River had had to see patients and hadn't been able to come to the breakfast. "Hi."

Jenny smiled. "Hi, darling. You look stunning. I meant to tell you all morning." Hazel wore a dress of her own creation. It had a simple cut, but only talent and skill could make satin simultaneously fit and fall like that.

"Thank you." Hazel smiled. "I brought a gift. Can I show you?"

"A gift for me?" Jenny pulled her chin back. "Sure. But...what's the occasion?" She followed Hazel to another table.

"The occasion is your wedding." Hazel lifted a bulky box from her chair.

"My wedding?"

Hazel smiled and looked around. "Is there anywhere more private we could go?"

"More private?" Jenny took a breath to center herself. What had Hazel done? "Of course. Um. Here, come with me." She waved the young woman to follow, leading the way out of the tasting room and upstairs into Jon's bachelor apartment. They had already furnished most of the new house but would use the apartment until the wedding.

Jenny closed the door to the staircase behind her and led Hazel into the living room. "Is this good?"

Her pretty guest nodded. "I only asked because..." She took a deep breath. "I hope you don't mind that I'm doing this."

Jenny folded her hands in front of her. "Do what?"

Hazel put the box on the coffee table and opened it, then pulled out a parcel and held it out. "I want you to have this wedding dress."

Jenny gazed at the soft package. The question of what the right thing to do was had lingered in her mind for a while. Eventually, she had made a decisive choice, closing the chapter on uncertainty. After the guests left and the buffet was cleared, she intended to approach Jon with a request—could they, perhaps, choose a simpler dress code for their wedding? Nothing extravagant, no white dress or tux. Just something elegant and tasteful, something they could wear again later.

Hazel was a wonderful dressmaker. No doubt about it.

But the last thing Jenny wanted was yet another wedding dress.

She cleared her throat. "You made me a dress?"

"I thought about making one myself. But I already had the perfect dress in my store. It's the same one you tried on."

Confused, Jenny blinked. "The one I tried on?"

Hazel nodded. "I know you fell in love with it."

"But..." Jenny set the package down on the table. "You promised your family not to sell me a dress."

"I am keeping my promise." Hazel smiled. "I'm not selling it to you. It's a gift. It's my wedding gift."

CHAPTER 32

J enny turned away, pretending that she had to switch on the light even though the room was perfectly bright.

It was a lovely gesture. Just like Hazel was a lovely person. Jenny couldn't wish for a better girlfriend for her son. But...

She turned back. "Hazel, thank you. I appreciate your offer. I really do. It's generous and considerate. I see all that."

Hazel set the parcel on the table. "But?"

Jenny sighed. "I just don't think I should walk down the aisle in a dress that wasn't meant for me."

"It *is* meant for you. I'm sure that's the reason it never sold." Hazel took a breath. "I hoped it could be your something gifted."

"Even if it's a present...it's just a way to get around the promise, isn't it? Everyone, from your great-grandmother to your mother, made you promise not to give me this dress. I'm all for keeping one's promises. What if you feel guilty later? I do not want to get in between you and your conscience."

"Of course you shouldn't wear it if you don't want to." Hazel leaned over the parcel, pulling the lavender ribbon loose. "As far as my conscience goes... All this time, it's been telling me one thing. You should wear the dress." The silk paper rustled, falling open. "Do you know about Robert and Marianne?"

And there was the dress. Shimmering champagne, perfection. Jenny blinked. "Yes. Audrey caught me up to speed. I was going to do some research after the wedding."

Hazel lifted the gown, unfurling its beauty.

It still was exactly what Jenny wanted Jon to see when she walked down the aisle. She still wanted to get married wearing a dress as beautiful and comfortable and easy as their love for each other. But how could she justify compromising Hazel for a few moments of vanity?

"Jenny, I'm breaking my promise on purpose," Hazel said softly. "I want to do it because it was wrong to ask me for it. I don't want to uphold a forgotten family feud that shouldn't exist in the first place."

Slowly, Jenny nodded. "I agree with that," she said quietly. "I don't want a feud either."

"So let's break the chain together. Let's make peace." Hazel smiled shyly. "The dress is yours if you want it." Carefully, she folded the gown back into the silk paper.

Jenny inhaled. "Then...thank you for the dress, and—thank you."

"I have something else for you." Hazel opened her satin satchel and pulled out a paper, handing it over.

"What is this?" Curiously, Jenny unfolded it.

"It's an article from an old newspaper," Hazel explained.

"What newspaper?"

"The Daily Courier; it went out of circulation a long time ago. A librarian helped me find the article on microfiche, and I had it printed out specially so the photo would show details."

"Yes, I see. Nice." It was a good copy, enhanced and printed with modern technology, the photo likely even clearer than in the original. Jenny's eyes flew over the heading and the first few lines. "This is about an award given to Herbert Whitman?"

"No." Hazel smiled. "The award was given to his wife. See? It says *Mrs*. Herbert Whitman."

"Mrs. Whitman." Jenny held the paper farther away. She really should start carrying the reading glasses she'd finally bought a week ago. "What about her?"

"She gave a speech at The International Paleontology Symposium of 1921."

"Was she a professor at my university?" Interest flicked through Jenny. She looked around, spotting the glasses on a side table. Quickly, she fetched them and put them on her nose. "Right. That's her in the photo, giving a speech. I don't remember ever coming across her name before."

Hazel shook her head. "Her husband was a professor at a university in Boston. His wife worked with him on his research into..." Hazel came over to read from the article. "Uh—the stratigraphic sequences of Devonian marine vertebrates." She straightened.

"It means that he worked on fossilized fish." Jenny looked closer at the photo. Slowly, puzzle pieces shifted into place. "Fossils, huh?"

Hazel smiled. "I looked up his publications. I don't understand much of what he writes, but he often mentions his wife's contributions. She wasn't a professor, but her research was important enough that it was acknowledged with an award at this conference."

"I'm glad. It was hard for female scientists back then." Jenny looked at Hazel over the brim of her glasses. "*Fossils*, huh?"

"Yes. Have another look at the woman in the photo."

Jenny lifted the article again, hope dawning in her heart. She wanted it to be true. She wanted Marianne's story to have a happy ending.

In the photo, the woman stood on the lectern. Because the photographer had situated themselves slightly behind and to the side of the speaker, only her bright smile was visible, with little of the rest of her face showing. Instead, the camera's attention was on the raptly listening audience.

Jenny felt a tug of disappointment. "Why couldn't they take a better photo of her? I want to see the face."

"I know. But look at the skirt."

Jenny leaned closer. Then she went to the window for better light. "Swirls? A big brooch pinned to her belt?"

"In the shape of ammonites," Hazel confirmed. "I think it's a golden pin Marianne mentions in her diary. Her mother had it made to hold up Marianne's skirts when she was hunting for fossils."

Jenny's eyes widened as she slowly began to believe. "Fossils *and* the pin—that's too many coincidences, isn't it? It really might be Marianne," she murmured. "Happily married, respected for her research, and giving a speech to fellow scientists." She felt her forehead crumple with relief. "Robert didn't get her after all."

"The article mentions her first name," Hazel said.

Jenny lowered her chin. "Where? What is it?"

"In this paragraph." Hazel showed her the lines. "It says Mary Anne Whitman."

Jenny's lips curled into a smile. "Mary Anne? That's really—oh! *Oh*!"

"What?"

"That's my grandmother Magda in the front row!" Jenny pointed and held the paper to the light again. "I have a photo of her; she looked just like me." She looked up. "Marianne's family knew where she was! They helped her get away from Robert." She exhaled, taking a moment to process. "I'm so glad," she whispered and closed her eyes. "I'm *so* glad. I was scared for her."

"I think her family was too. But they made sure Robert wouldn't find her to take revenge," Hazel murmured. "Marianne left the cove for a new life in Boston." She looked up. "Jenny?"

"Yes?"

Hazel cleared her throat. "I apologize for what Robert did to your family. I wish Marianne could have stayed."

"Don't apologize, darling. You didn't do anything." Jenny took Hazel's hands into her own. "Who knows what doors Marianne opened for herself by leaving? If she had stayed, she might never have met the love of her life or fulfilled her dreams." She smiled. "You know... I'm starting to think Marianne would want me to wear this wedding dress. I really do."

Hazel lowered her head. "Thank you, Jenny."

Jenny let go of Hazel's hands only to pull the young woman into her arms. "Thank *you*, darling. It takes courage to break free from generational patterns. Especially those we carry without knowing it."

"Mom once said that every generation knows a little more and does a little better. If I'd had a chance to tell her about Robert and Marianne, I'm sure she would have agreed with me."

"I'm sure she would have," Jenny murmured, touched by Hazel's longing for her mother. Quietly, she promised herself to always be there for the young woman.

EPILOGUE

D o you think Jenny will ever come downstairs?" Faye took a bite of the slice of poppyseed cake she'd snuck from the kitchen of the old hotel.

Hazel smiled to herself. It wouldn't be a proper wedding without nerves. After everyone had gotten dressed and their hair done upstairs, Jenny had asked for a moment alone to collect herself. Her friends had fluttered downstairs to drink lemonade and nibble on cake while they waited for their bride.

"Of course she will. She has to. She's getting married, isn't she?" Billie blew out a tense breath. "We all know Jenny's a special little starfish, but she has to—*oof*. I can hear her steps. Finally." She hurried to stand with the other bridesmaids.

A moment later, Jenny appeared on the sweeping steps in Marianne's dress like a vision of past and present, of old and young, of love and memories.

"Here," Hazel whispered when Jenny reached the floor, and she handed her the bouquet. "You look fantastic."

Jenny smiled a small thanks before Billy started to tell her who was sitting where, waiting for them outside.

"Hazel, can you snip this thread here real quick?" Ava lifted the skirt of her blue dress, where an errant thread had so far escaped notice.

"Sure." Hazel pulled out her small silver scissors and cut off the offender. "Any other wardrobe emergencies?"

"Nope. Mine's perfect," Faye said happily and let her skirt swish from side to side. "Once all this is over, I'm ordering a couple of maternity dresses from you. That is, if you have time to make them before I pop."

"Of course I have time. Just stop by the store." Hazel tucked her kit away and surveyed the gathered bridesmaids. They each wore their own preferred style of dress, but Hazel had sewn them all in the same light, breezy, sapphire blue material that complemented the colors of the cove and the ocean. The effect was lovely when they stood next to Jenny in her shimmering champagne-colored silk.

"You all look gorgeous," Hazel declared. "My work here is done." She nodded at Billie.

"Ready?" Billie put her hands on Jenny's shoulders and gazed deep into her eyes. "You're not going to pass out, are you? Even Gabe managed to get through his vows."

"Hey," Faye protested. She popped the last bite of her slice of cake into her mouth and brushed a crumb off her fingers. "Gabe was fine. Solid as a rock."

"How about you, Jenny?" Ava asked, smiling. "Do you feel solid as a rock?"

"Uh." Jenny exhaled. "Yeah."

"Excellent." Billie nodded toward the patio. "Jon went outside ten minutes ago. We should probably... Also, it's *hot* in here, isn't it?" She fanned herself with her hand.

"It's cooler outside," Hazel promised. Billie was a bit pale around the nose herself with the excitement of her brother and best friend tying the knot.

"I'm ready." Jenny moistened her lips.

Faye eyed Jenny thoughtfully. "You and Jon couldn't have asked for a more beautiful evening."

Jenny nodded.

"Uh-oh, girls, she's stopped talking." Faye took Jenny's hand and walked her to the open French door that was veiled with a gauzy white curtain. "Just come after us, okay? All the way to the front where Jon is."

"Yes."

"Can you do that? Jenny?"

Jenny swallowed with difficulty. "Yes. Yes, I can do that. Let's go. I think I'm going to drown in butterflies if we wait any longer."

Billie smiled. "He's feeling the same. Hazel, we're ready."

"Good luck." Hazel went out onto the patio and sent a quick text. A moment later, the sweet melody of an old waltz drifted over the beach. Hazel slipped into her chair next to River.

He took her hand, holding it between his own. "Everything all right?" he whispered.

"Yes." She smiled at him. "Your mother looks stunning."

He mouthed a thank-you and turned to wait for the bride's entrance.

Hazel glanced at Jon. The handsome vintner in his tuxedo waited calmly under an archway made of green vines, fragrant jasmine, and blooming peonies. Behind him, the sea lapped at the beach like a curious kitten.

She turned, looking toward the hotel. This was an entrance she did want to witness.

The billowing white curtains formed a graceful gateway, and one after the other, the bridesmaid emerged from it in their blue silk gowns, as joyful and radiant as middle-aged water nymphs.

Finally, Jenny stepped out.

A gasp of admiration went through the seated guests.

Slowly, Jenny walked toward Jon, her dress flowing in the sea breeze, the delicate lace and silk shimmering in the light of the evening. Her long blonde hair hung down in soft, loose curls, cascading around her shoulders like liquid gold. Her butterflies seemed to be forgotten, and when she reached Jon, her radiant smile mirrored his. He held out his hand to take hers, their fingers entwined in silent promise, and they shared a brief smile before turning to the officiant.

Billie arranged the silken train, and the officiant started to speak.

River's grip on Hazel's hand suddenly tightened. She put a hand on his arm and leaned closer. "You okay?" she whispered.

River looked at her, then tucked a strand of her hair behind her ear. "I love you," he murmured. He lifted her hand to his mouth and kissed her fingers.

"I love you too, River." Her breath barely carried the words.

For a brief moment, their eyes locked. Then River smiled, and they turned to watch the vows.

Each word the couple spoke was filled with honesty and passion, promising to be there for each other no matter what life brought their way. Somewhere in the middle of the vows, River handed Hazel a tissue. Smiling, she took it and dabbed her eyes.

Had it been up to her, the ceremony on the lovely, warm beach could have gone on forever. Much too soon, the couple exchanged rings as a symbol of their commitment to one another and Jon pulled Jenny close to kiss her, sealing their union.

"That was beautiful," River murmured as the guests erupted in cheers.

"It was," Hazel agreed. "One of the most beautiful weddings I've seen."

Music began to play from an unseen source, soft strings filling the air with their joyful melody. Under the flowers, Jenny looked up at Jon, who smiled, cradled her cheek, whispered something meant only for her, and kissed her again.

Together, the newlyweds walked down the aisle toward their future, hand in hand, to the applause of their friends and family.

River and Hazel joined the milling crowd. The October sun was sinking quickly, and the first stars started to glitter in the plum-colored sky. The lanterns and fairy lights lining the beach slowly flickered to life, illuminating the warm sand with their glow.

"Darlings!" Jenny emerged from a bauble of well-wishers and came to meet River and Hazel.

"Congratulations, Mom." River kissed his mother's cheek. "You look stunning."

"Thanks to Hazel," Jenny said and smiled warmly at her, then put a hand on her son's arm. "Listen, I'm going to cut the cake with Jon. River, before I forget again... Do you remember my friend Christy? She was in the process of buying a seaside cottage in the cove."

"She was visiting when I first arrived." River nodded. "She talked about renovating the place herself."

"Well, I think the sale should have happened by now. She's helped us with the heirlooms, and I was wondering if you would offer our help in turn with the renovations. I don't know when she was planning to start; I meant to call her yesterday, but I had too much going on."

"No problem, Mom. I'll find her and make sure she knows we're here for her," River promised.

"Thank you, darling." Jenny smiled. "She came with her friends, Agatha and Barbara. You can't miss them." Jenny hugged River and kissed Hazel's cheek, then looked up at someone waving from the crowd. "Oh, there's Audrey! I haven't talked to her yet."

"Go ahead, Mom. I'll find you later," River said. Jenny waved and was gone, swept up by a wave of friends toward her daughter.

"I think the cake has to wait a while longer." Hazel nodded at the four-tier, beach-themed masterpiece that had magically appeared on a table in the middle of the patio and was guarded by a stern-looking Hannah.

"I'm starving," River said longingly. "I've been working up to the last minute. It's been a bit of a rush today."

Hazel smiled at him. "We should talk about work-life balance one of these days."

"I couldn't agree more." River smiled back. "I do need much more time with you. But until then, how about we find Christy, Agatha, and...who?"

"Barbara," Hazel helped him out. "I've never met her, but I hear she's fabulously wealthy and lives in an old estate that is as magnificent as it is mysterious."

"Barbara." River pulled Hazel's arm through his own and squared his shoulders. "Let's go talk to them. I'm curious what they are up to with their abandoned seaside cottages and mysterious mansions."

"Me too." Hazel smiled, her heart full of love for this man, the beauty of the starlit beach, this marvelous moment in time. "They're probably involved in a whole saga of secrets." She sighed happily. "Oh look! There they are."

Thank you so much for reading! Stay in beautiful Mendocino Cove and read **A Saga of Secrets and Sisters**!

MENDOCINO COVE SERIES

★★★★★ *"I loved it all, the history, the mystery, the sea, the love of family and friends...!"*
A gorgeous feel-good series with wonderful characters! Four friends are taking a second chance on love and life as they start over together in the small town of Mendocino Cove. Set on the breathtakingly beautiful coast of Northern California, where the golden hills are covered in wildflowers, vineyards grow sweet grapes, and the coast is rugged and wild.

Bay Harbor Beach Series

★★★★★ *"Wonderfully written story. Rumors abound in this tale of loves and secrets."*
Lose yourself in this riveting feel-good saga of old secrets and new beginnings. Best friends support each other through life's ups and downs and matters of the heart as they boil salt water taffy, browse quaint stores for swimsuits, and sample pies at the Beach Bistro!

BEACH COVE SERIES

★★★★★ *"What an awesome series! Captivated in the first sentence! Beautiful writing!"*

Maisie returns to charming Beach Cove and meets a heartwarming cast of old friends and new neighbors. The beaches are sandy and inviting, the sea is bluer than it should be, and the small town is brimming with big secrets. Together, Maisie and her sisters of the heart take turns helping each other through trials, mysteries, and matters of the heart.

ABOUT THE AUTHOR

Nellie Brooks writes feel-good friendship fiction for women. In her books you'll find flawed, likable characters who bake and adopt animals, gorgeous coastal settings that will make you study your tea leaves for the next vacation date, secrets that are best solved together, and happy endings until every estranged friend and distant sister is safe in the arms of her small town community.

Visit www.nelliebrooks.com to subscribe to her newsletter and hear about releases, promos, and writing news! You can also follow Nellie on Facebook and BookBub.

Made in United States
North Haven, CT
08 August 2024

55818120R00159